The EDELWEISS ✳ Pirates

DIRK REINHARDT

TRANSLATED FROM THE
GERMAN BY RACHEL WARD

INTRODUCTION BY MICHAEL ROSEN

PUSHKIN PRESS

Pushkin Press
71–75 Shelton Street
London WC2H 9JQ

Original text © Aufbau Verlag GmbH & Co. KG, Berlin 2012
English translation © Rachel Ward 2021
Introduction © Michael Rosen 2021

The Edelweiss Pirates was first published as *Edelweisspiraten*
by Aufbau Verlag GmbH & Co in Berlin, 2012

First published by Pushkin Press in 2021

The translation of this work was supported by
a grant from the Goethe-Institut

3 5 7 9 8 6 4 2

ISBN 13: 978-1-78269-309-3

Cover image © NS-Documentation Centre
of the City of Cologne, Germany

Designed and typeset by Tetragon, London
Printed and bound by CPI Group (UK) Ltd, Croydon, CR0 4YY

www.pushkinpress.com

In memory of

Jean Jülich
(18.4.1929–19.10.2011)

Fritz Theilen
(27.9.1927–18.4.2012)

INTRODUCTION

In 2001 I travelled to Cologne (Köln) in Germany to help make a radio programme about the Edelweiss Pirates. At the time, all I knew about them came from a few articles that I had read: a mix of personal accounts of what old men had said or written and a few rather difficult scholarly articles on what historians thought about these "Pirates".

When I arrived in Germany and began talking to people, things started to become clear. During the Second World War, in Cologne and other areas in the west of Germany especially, groups of young people had gathered together in groups or gangs. These groups weren't an organized movement like, say, the Boy Scouts. In fact, they were opposed to the organized movements in Germany at the time: the Hitler Youth and the girls' organization, the BDM. As we talked, it was clear that over the years of the Nazi regime or "Third Reich" (1933–1945) these Pirates changed. What started out as a rejection of the Hitler Youth, became more clearly an opposition to the special fanatic security forces of the Third Reich, the Gestapo and the SS.

So it was, in the early days, the Pirates loved to meet informally in parks, in the woods, up in the mountains. They would play guitar and sing folk songs, as well as parodies of Hitler Youth songs, with the lyrics changed to insult the Nazi regime.

One man who had been a Pirate showed us the park where they used to meet. He told us that one day he had seen his father go by: he was in a forced labour gang. He had been arrested right at the beginning of the Third Reich because he had been a representative in a trade union. We talked to him some of the time in the very building where he had been held by the security forces and roughed up. I think it may well be the very same building that you'll read about in this book.

You'll also see why these young people called themselves Edelweiss Pirates. I won't spoil anything by saying why. However, some details about Germany and the war might be useful if you don't know much about it.

Before the Nazis rose to power, Germany was a fully democratic country, electing MPs in much the same way as we do in the UK. Economically, things were not going well for millions of Germans, just as they weren't going well in Great Britain, France and the USA. The Nazi Party became the largest party in Germany but not bigger than all the other parties, and not bigger than the sum of the two parties most opposed to them, the Socialists and the Communists. This tells us that ordinary German people were very divided on how to get out of the economic difficulty. In the first months of 1933, the leader of the Nazis, Adolf Hitler, and the most senior members of that party—people like Goebbels, Goering and Himmler, names you will come across in this book—seized power. They passed two laws which meant that Hitler became a dictator and Germany was run as a "totalitarian state". Everything was run by the Nazi Party and its militarized security forces. The justice system was brought under Nazi control, and all political organizations apart from the Nazi Party were banned. Freedom of speech through newspapers, radio, magazines and books came to an end. What people call "terror" came to be used as a means of ruling over ordinary people in their everyday lives. Trusted sympathizers of the Nazis were encouraged to spy on people who might be "untrustworthy" or not loyal to the "Fatherland"—the name used to describe Germany.

The terror was used to persecute people. Sometimes this was done on political grounds, while at other times it was motivated by the Nazis' ideas about race, sexuality, and physical and mental capability. One of the reasons they rose to power was because they had created a part-political, part-mythological view of the human race in which people they described as "Aryan" (white northern-Europeans) were superior to everyone else and that some other peoples in particular were *Untermenschen* or "subhuman": especially Jews, people of colour, "gypsies" (Roma, Sinti and all nomadic peoples) and people with severe mental illness. They also persecuted people who they deemed to have the "wrong" sexuality, in particular gay men. From 1933 to 1945, there was a slide from persecution, terror and imprisonment to murder, to mass murder or what is called "genocide". There was a calculated, deliberate, scientific and industrialized attempt to wipe out all the Jews and "gypsies" from wherever the Nazis ruled, as well as millions of other civilians in Eastern Europe and the Soviet Union. When Nazism was finally defeated in 1945, the death toll from this barbarism was around fifteen million—in addition to all those who were killed or wounded on the battlefields and seas where the war was waged.

But what was life like for ordinary German people in that period? Mostly, when people from the countries that were opposed to the Nazis write about this time, the attitudes, activities and everyday lives of Germans are not their main interest. The billions of words written are mostly spent looking at, for example, the rise to power of the Nazis, the persecution, the genocide, the battles, the spying, the bombing and the last days of the Nazi regime. Much is written about the Nazi leaders, in particular Hitler himself. It's been said, in rather a cynical and gruesome way, that if you want to sell a book, put a swastika on the cover. The swastika, you'll probably know, is the symbol that the Nazis "borrowed" from ancient Indian culture to put on their flags and uniforms.

Meanwhile, the lives of ordinary Germans tend to get obscured. Sometimes people make claims about what

German people thought about the Nazis without necessarily backing it up with eyewitness accounts. Often the picture we are given is that all German people were united behind Hitler and the Nazi atrocities and the Nazi drive to war. Sometimes very small acts of resistance are mentioned only to show that there was no "mass" resistance to the Nazis. You'll catch sight of these small acts in this book: the White Rose and the plot to assassinate Hitler. The Edelweiss Pirates don't often get a mention. Why not?

I think that's partly because they were young people (under the age of twenty-one) and partly because they weren't an organized force. They were young people who knew what they didn't like without writing out demands or manifestos or demonstrating in the conventional way. They lived their resistance through style, music, difference and by not belonging. That said, by the end of the war, things in Cologne started to get more serious. Again, I don't want to spoil the story that unfolds in this book, but one measure of how seriously the Nazis took the Edelweiss Pirates is the punishment meted out to them: beatings, arrests, torture and even prison camps.

In 1945, when the war ended, Germany was a crushed, defeated, smashed country. Millions of people were hungry, the country was occupied by foreign forces (the "allies" who had defeated them). The country was divided into "zones" which eventually became two sides—East and West. But for all Germans there followed a mental and social struggle to understand what had happened. As a country, the world condemned them for the crimes of genocide and stirring up war through invasion. In this book you will meet an old man who feels that he hasn't had the space to tell the story of what it was like to be young, struggling to be free and full of fun at the time of the Third Reich.

I hope you'll find it a fascinating, moving, tense read—just as I did.

MICHAEL ROSEN
November 2020

The

EDELWEISS

✻

Pirates

The images stay with me. They won't let me go. It was three days ago now that they murdered my brother. But I can still see it before my eyes, every second.

Tom and Flint didn't want me to go. They were afraid something might happen to me. Thought the Gestapo would recognize me and nab me. But I didn't listen to them. I had to go. In the end, they gave in and came too, to make sure I didn't do anything stupid at least.

It was in Hüttenstrasse. Where they've been executing people for a month or two now. Outside Ehrenfeld station.

By the time we arrived, the square was already full. Gawpers everywhere, drawn in by the posters. Dull faces, greedy for sensation. We mixed in with them. Right outside the station, there was the gallows. Two long cross-beams, resting on a frame. The bottom one for their feet, the nooses thrown over the top one.

I saw Mum further forwards. Two women were holding her up. I badly wanted to run over to her, but Tom and Flint held me back. There were Gestapo spies everywhere. Standing there, looking inconspicuous. Listening out for anyone saying the wrong things. Lurking in wait for people like us, who're on the wanted lists. We kept our heads down and pulled our hoods over our faces.

After a few minutes, the SS marched up. When I saw them with their machine guns, all my hopes crumbled. I'd been secretly playing with the idea of rescuing my brother. But it was no good. The only weapons I had were an old knife and one of our basic Molotov cocktails.

Mum turned around, as if she was searching for me. She looked scared and desperate. Helpless. Kind of against my will, I shoved my hand in my pocket and gripped the knife. Maybe I should go, I thought. Now—before it's too late.

But then the lorry arrived with the prisoners. They were sitting in the back, which was uncovered, their hands tied behind them. Horst was there too. He was wearing his SS uniform, but the badges he used to be so proud of had been ripped off. They dragged him and the others to the gallows. He kept his head down and climbed onto the beam. One of the SS men put the noose round his neck while he just stared blankly into space.

Right away, one of the Gestapo men read out the death warrant. I couldn't take it in. Just stared at Horst. My brother! Who'd always been so strong. The one I admired. Now the noose was round his neck. But at the moment I looked at him, he suddenly raised his head. Like he was trying to find me.

I let go of the knife and grabbed the Moli. What if I light it and lob it so it goes off among all the SS? I thought. Maybe they'd panic? Maybe I could rescue Horst in the mayhem and then we could...

But before I had time to do anything, Tom was there. He must've been watching me. Probably guessed what I was planning. He grabbed my hand and held on tight.

I crumpled and shut my eyes. He was right. I knew it, but I didn't want it to be true. We stood there like that for a couple of seconds, then a murmur went round the crowd. I didn't need to look to know why: the SS had started the executions. One by one, the nooses would be jerked tight, the prisoners would lose their balance on the beam and kick the air, fighting with death. Same hideous show every time.

When I opened my eyes again, Horst was still standing there, but the man next to him was just being pulled up in the air, so he'd be next. I couldn't bear it and tried to get away from Tom. But Flint appeared on the other side of me. He grabbed me, put his hand over my mouth and nodded to Tom. Then they dragged me away.

Over the people's heads, I saw my brother being yanked up in the air. And I heard Mum cry out. I reared up, wanted to shake Tom and Flint off. But they held me tight, trying to pull me away before anyone noticed us.

At some point, I stopped fighting. Horst was dead because he saved us. It was like part of me had died up there.

It all began when I wouldn't let somebody go. Would he have stayed of his own accord? Probably not. He was too shy for that.

It was two months ago. I was standing at my grandfather's grave not long after he died. The sky was bleak and grey; everywhere, the last leaves were falling from the trees. I stood there, missing him, the way I still miss him. I often went to see him—before. If there was something I couldn't deal with. He was so relaxed. Nothing fazed him. No matter what was on my mind, if I discussed it with him, I felt after a while as though it was small and unimportant and didn't actually matter at all.

It was gradually getting dark; I was about to go. Then I noticed this old man, a short distance away, by one of the other graves. There was nothing special about him. But I'd been there the week before, and the week before that, and every time, I'd seen him in exactly that spot. I looked more closely at him and could see that his lips were moving, as if he were talking to someone—but there was nobody around. There was only the gravestone by his feet.

And I noticed something else. He kept looking over at me. He wasn't paying any attention to anybody else.

Whenever he raised his head, he looked at me, and nobody else. I didn't know what to make of it. It was a bit creepy.

After a while, he turned and walked away. As I watched him, I suddenly had a feeling that I should ask him about the way he was acting. I'm not normally like that, but that day I felt an urge and before it faded, I'd run after him. It was quite a way to the grave he'd been standing by, but he walked very slowly, with small steps, cautiously feeling his way, so he hadn't got far when I reached it.

"Excuse me!" I called after him.

He stopped and turned around.

"Excuse me," I said again. "Do we know each other, by any chance?"

He looked uncertainly at me. "No. I-I don't think so."

"It's just that—you kept looking over at me. So, I thought, maybe we'd met but I just didn't recognize you."

"Oh!" He seemed embarrassed. "You noticed that, then?"

"Well, I don't know about noticed, I just kind of wondered."

He came hesitantly closer. "Yes, you're right, I was looking at you. I was wondering why a young person like you keeps coming here. It's the third time I've seen you now. You should be—I don't know—playing football or something."

So that was it; he'd just been curious. Or was there more to it? When I looked at him, I couldn't shake off the feeling that he had only told me half the truth. He looked away and turned around, as if to leave… but then he didn't. An embarrassing silence was building up. To stop it going on too long, I pointed at the grave we were standing next to.

"Is that—a relative of yours?"

"Yes," he said. "My brother. Today is the sixty-seventh anniversary of his death."

I took a closer look at the gravestone. "Horst Gerlach", it read. And beneath it: "18.2.1925–24.11.1944". Then I realized. Today was the 24th of November!

"Was he killed in the war?" I asked.

"No. He was murdered."

It sounded strange, the way he said that. I wondered whether everyone who died in war was somehow "murdered"—at least in some way or other.

"It's a long story," he said when I didn't reply. "But it might interest you. *You especially!*"

I was only listening with half an ear. Standing by his brother's gravestone were three red memorial candles, which were all lit, and lying next to them were flowers. White flowers.

"If you'd like to hear it, I'll tell you," he continued. "What do you think? You could come to my place."

I hesitated. We didn't know each other. Why was he inviting me to his place? I must have looked pretty astonished, because he cringed.

"No," he said hastily. "No, that was stupid of me. Please, forget I said it, OK?"

The next moment, he turned and walked away. I hadn't meant that to happen. I raised my hand and wanted to call out to him—but by then that sudden feeling, the one that had made me run after him, had disappeared. Instead I just watched until he was out of sight, and then I walked away too.

On my way home, there was one thing I couldn't get out of my mind. He'd stressed it so emphatically. What had he meant—this story might interest *me especially?*

12th March 1941

It's finally happened. It had been building up for months and today it went off with a bang. Tom and me and the others got into a scrap with Morken and his lot, and there was a punch-up you could hear the other side of Cologne. I'm still black and blue. Don't care though: Morken's lot look worse.

It'd been brewing for months. Over a year. Since the war started. Loads of the older Hitler Youth leaders volunteered for the army. Since then we've been bossed around by the Platoon Leaders and they're only fourteen or fifteen—hardly any older than us. But they're all from the grammar school. So much for everyone in the HJ being treated the same and having the same chances—it's a fairy tale. You learn that fast. They'd never dream of making one of us common boys from Klarastrasse a leader. In the end, they always pick the ones from the posh schools, with the rich fathers.

They despise us. In their eyes, we're riff-raff, scum— they don't mix with the likes of us. So they bully us into the ground at the Hitler Youth, the HJ. Morken's the worst. His dad's some rich factory owner with the right Party membership. He's been the Platoon Leader for a few months and fancies himself as a little general. Makes us stand to attention for hours or crawl through the mud in the rain.

On the training evenings, we have to read out essays and he and his cronies laugh at how stupid we are. They never miss an opportunity to prove they're better than us.

Which is why I'm sick of HJ duties now. Back before the war, it was better. But now: march, fall in, drill, fall in again, more marching. Always the same. And if anyone gets it wrong, he has to do pack drill, like in the army. Morken's always thinking up new dirty tricks. Course they're only for us, never his lot.

We're meant to be learning "military virtues". But that's the last thing Tom and me and the other lads from round here want. Life's nothing but drill and doing as you're told anyway: first at home, then at school, then at work. We get bossed around and pushed around everywhere. We really don't need any more.

But the worst is all the talk about "a hero's death". Dad was killed in the war last year. Morken's old man isn't even fighting and nor are the other posh boys' dads. They know how to get out of it. And then Morken pops up at a training evening and drones on about how there's nothing more beautiful than dying a hero's death for our country, for Führer and Fatherland. With that mocking look in his eye! It makes me long to throttle him every time.

Anyway, a week or two back, I started skiving off. And me and Tom always do everything together, so he skived too. We kept thinking up new excuses, why we couldn't come. Course everyone knew they were a pack of lies. Morken was blue in the face at losing his favourite victims.

*The other day, a written warning came in the post.
There'd be "serious consequences" if we didn't turn up
right away. We couldn't think of any more excuses, so today
we went.*

*That was what Morken had been waiting for. He was
in his element all right. Ordered us to crawl through the
mushy snow as a punishment for skiving. But we'd already
decided there was no way we'd make idiots of ourselves. So
we said no.*

*Morken was speechless. Refusing to obey orders is the
worst crime in the HJ. They wouldn't care if you killed
your own mum, but insubordination is right out. He said
it again, and we refused again. So he ordered the whole
platoon to pile on me and Tom and beat us up. That's
actually against the rules but it still happens now and then.*

*But it didn't go the way Morken planned. The lads
from our road stood up to him. So instead of a pile on, there
was a massive punch-up between the riff-raff and Morken's
lot. All the stored-up hate came bursting out. Nobody gave
a damn about the HJ or ranks or orders or anything.*

*Revenge can sure as hell taste sweet. We'd been longing
to do that for months, and now we have.*

15th March 1941

*Today, Tom and I had to go and see the Jungstammführer.
About the business on Wednesday. Course the HJ won't just*

put up with stuff like that. Specially cos word got out about it.

When we arrived, Morken was already there. He explained how it all happened. Hammed it right up of course. You'd have thought we were serious criminals, Tom and me. Double murder at least. After that, we were allowed to speak too. Didn't really bother though. Cos nobody would believe us anyway.

The Jungstammführer, a funny, pale lad, two or three years older than us, listened to it all. It seemed like he mostly wanted to avoid a fuss. Probably cos he knew a punishment beating's against the rules really. Anyway, in the end, he decided we should officially apologize to Morken and our platoon. And that was that.

Me and Tom, we looked at each other and both had the same thought. Apologize to Morken? Never! Over our dead bodies! So we refused.

The Jungstammführer, who probably thought he'd been extra lenient, couldn't believe his ears. He loomed over us and whacked us one each. But that only made us more determined and stubborn. In the end, he threw us out, announcing that he'd think up some "special treatment" just for us.

When we got home, we tried to top each other's ideas of what we'd do to Morken if we met him in the street. Make him lick the slush off the pavement? Tar and feather him? Set his feet in concrete and drop him in the sewers? Just as well we didn't see him.

30th March 1941

That's it. Over and done. Goodbye HJ! There's no going back for me and Tom now.

Since going to the Jungstammführer, we've had a few "absolutely final" warnings to turn up for duty again. But we didn't. We swore never to go back to the HJ. No more crawling in the mud and being bossed around by people like Morken, or anyone else. No matter what they do to us.

Today is the last Sunday in March, so it's time for the big coming-of-age ceremony. After four years in the Jungvolk, members of the German Youth take a pledge and graduate to the Hitler Youth. Standing there with torches listening to thousands of speeches. Tom and me were meant to go too. But we didn't want to.

Course we had a bad feeling about it. Everyone says you get in massive trouble if you leave the HJ. But who knows? Maybe it's just talk. Perhaps they just want to scare you and it's not actually that bad. Cos what can they do? They can't kill us, we're too young for the army, we've got nothing they could take away and we're used to boxed ears.

So what've they got left?

3rd April 1941

Yesterday was our last day of school. Eight years of compulsory education over. We're fourteen now, Tom and me.

Old enough to serve Führer and Fatherland as part of the workforce.

I'm glad to be done with school and so's Tom. Mostly cos of Kriechbaum. Seven years we had him as our teacher. The one before him was OK. We liked him, he wasn't as grim. But he left and we got Kriechbaum. Must have been in '34 or thereabouts.

Everything changed with him. First, we had to learn the Führer's life story by heart. And then, every morning we had to stand ramrod straight and yell "Heil Hitler!"

We didn't take it all that seriously at first, found it funny if anything, but Kriechbaum was the wrong bloke to try that with. One lunchtime, he had us fall in after the last lesson and everyone had to do the salute. You were only allowed to go if you did it right. Everyone else had to do it again. Me and Tom had to have about ten goes before we finally got out of there. But two other boys from our road, whose parents wouldn't let them do the Hitler salute, dug their heels in. Kriechbaum could do what he liked, they just stood there with their gobs shut.

We'd probably have laughed about it, except that the results were no fun. From then on, Kriechbaum would call "the Klarastrasse lot" up to the front at least once a week—including me and Tom—and thrash us in front of the class, whether we'd done anything to deserve it or not. You could guarantee it.

Getting a thrashing was nothing new, mind you. Our dads gave us those too. But at least they had a reason—or

*tried to find one. Kriechbaum just did it cos we were
from working families on Klarastrasse who were too
stupid to even know the Hitler salute. That was all. We
hated him. And by the end, we couldn't stand anything
about school.*

*But now we're rid of the bloke. It's a good feeling. No
more Kriechbaum! No more Morken! No more thrashings,
no stupid drills. Some days, you just feel free and easy.
Today's one of them.*

1st May 1941

*May Day! Labour Day—that's a bad joke! I've spent three
weeks running my feet off from one factory to another,
getting nowhere. Really need some money. Since Dad died
and Horst's been at that school in Bavaria, we've been
stony broke. Got debts everywhere, can hardly pay the rent.
Tom and his mum are the same. So we're desperately trying
to get a place.*

*Problem is, no one wants us. Everyone else from our
class got an apprenticeship ages ago. Well—everyone in
the HJ, that is. It's pretty obvious. Wherever we turn up,
we might as well not bother. They won't even talk to us.
As if we've got the plague or something. We're starting to
realize: that's what they meant by "trouble".*

*Mum's narked. The last couple of days, she's been
trudging round all the factories that didn't want me. Told*

them her husband died serving the Fatherland and they
can't go making life harder for her son now too. She won't
stand for it and we bloody well deserve decent treatment.
Pretty brave of her. But it didn't do any good.

So we're pretty screwed. What if it goes on like this? If I
really can't get anything? What'll happen to us then?

9th May 1941

It all happened pretty fast in the end. I found an
apprenticeship at Ostermann and Flüs. Where Dad
worked. Back before the war. They make ship propellers.
"The largest ship propellers in the world," Dad always
said. They're right here in Ehrenfeld, on Grünerweg, not
far from our flat.

One or two of Dad's old colleagues must've put a good
word in for me. Any rate, I got to go and see the personnel
manager this morning, to sign my contract. I was in a
good mood cos it'd finally happened. But that soon faded
when I got in there. The way he looked at me made me feel
quite different, and I soon saw that I'd have to be careful
around him.

First he made me stand at his desk. Acted like I wasn't
there, just scribbled on his papers the whole time. But then,
after ten minutes or so, he leant back and looked me over
from head to toe.

"D'you know why we're taking you, Gerlach?"

"No. I don't actually."

"Didn't think you'd have the brains to work it out. So I'll tell you, we're taking you because your father worked here. Did good and reliable work. For many years. That's the only reason. It's got nothing to do with you, got that?"

"Yes, got that."

"I should hope so. I'll tell you just one thing, if you have any respect for your father, pull your damn socks up and don't disgrace him." He looked at me and shook his head. "Bloody hell, how did the man end up with a little toerag like you? He really deserved better!"

I thought I'd better not answer. He left me to sweat and leafed through his papers. Then he looked up again.

"Know why I called you a little toerag?"

"No."

"Of course not! You don't even know your own name. So, I'll tell you: you're a little toerag because you're not in the HJ any more. And why aren't you?"

"Well, there was some trouble and—"

"Shut your stupid mouth or I'll throw you out and then you can see where you end up! Don't think for a moment you can get away with murder just because your father worked here! And one more thing: the trouble didn't just happen on its own. You caused trouble! Didn't you?"

I was pleased they'd taken me on and determined to make a good impression. So I agreed with him.

"Yes, I caused trouble."

"What was that? Speak up a bit, can't you?"

"YES, I CAUSED TROUBLE!"

He slapped his hand on the desk with a bang. "What are you thinking of, yelling like that in here? Watch your step or you'll get a box round the ear!"

He left me standing there again and scribbled on his papers. Then he picked one up and slapped it down in front of me.

"Here, sign your contract, idiot!"

I didn't need telling twice. He snatched it out of my hand almost before I'd finished.

"Good grief, I really don't know why we go to so much bother for little toerags like you! Now get out of here and report to the foundry. And you'd better not let me see you up here again, or you really will be in the shit!"

I knew apprentices were pretty much the lowest of the low, but I didn't think it'd be that bad. Never mind! The main thing is, I've got a contract and I'm earning my own money, even if it isn't much. Walking through the streets today, I felt like people were looking at me differently, which is a load of nonsense of course—but it felt good anyway.

14th May 1941

Got through my first few days as an apprentice. Some of the instructors treat me like an old cleaning rag, but lots of the workers are nice. Specially the ones who knew Dad. I'm well in with them. They like me. They keep saying I remind them of him. They might just be saying that, but they might not. Anyway, I like to hear it. And the others can sod off.

One of the older blokes, who was a friend of Dad's, sort of looks out for me. Today, at lunch, he told me I hadn't really needed to worry about finding work. The HJ just want to make people like me think a bit. Hang us out to dry for a while so we see sense. In the long run, they can't do without us in the factories while there's a war on. Course he only told me in secret.

The work's pretty tough and takes longer than it should. It was already dark by the time I got away today. Then I always walk down Vogelsanger Strasse and over Neptunplatz, past the swimming pool. Normally there's nobody around at that time but today was different. There was a group of lads hanging around, about my age or a bit older. Making a right racket. Almost like the whole square belonged to them. I stopped and watched them from a distance. And then I remembered that I'd heard about people like them back in the HJ.

The patrols used to talk about them. Since last year, they've been pretty busy cos young people aren't allowed out after dark any more, and the patrols are meant to check up on them. They're allowed to ask for their papers and make arrests. At any rate, they were all talking about it in front of us younger ones. About what happened last night and their heroic deeds. How they'd swept some "shady characters", some load of "filth" or "scum" off the streets and chased them away.

Back then, Tom and I wondered why the shady characters needed chasing away every week. And why the patrols sometimes ended up with bruised faces. And then a couple of boys whispered to us they'd heard a different story. They'd heard that the patrols here in Ehrenfeld had taken a real beating again. Which was why they weren't coming round this way at night any more. And that the guys who'd done that to them weren't afraid of anything.

Making fun of the flag anthem for example. The HJ's sacred anthem! They don't sing, "Our banner flutters before us, we enter the future man for man." They sing, "Our Baldur flutters before us, our Baldur is a chubby man." They mean the ex-Reich Youth Leader, of course. Baldur von Schirach. Apparently, they call him—and the lads who told us really whispered this bit—"Baldur von Stink-Arse". We didn't know whether to believe them, Tom and me. Anyone who tried that in the HJ would've been beaten half-dead.

Anyway, now I'm wondering if those lads at the Neptune Pool might've been them. They were noisy enough. And they looked like the patrol described them. I'd really love to know!

16th May 1941

Tom's signed his apprenticeship contract too now, just a few days after I did. He's training to be a boilermaker at Klöckner-Humboldt-Deutz, over the other side of the Rhine. I told him about the people I saw at the Neptune Pool, and we went over there together after work today. We hung about the place and waited. And yes! When it got dark, they appeared again. Almost like ghosts, we didn't even see them coming.

At first we were a bit scared. But then we really wanted to know what they actually do and what they talk about. So we crept up to them. Keeping in the shadows so they wouldn't notice. But I reckon they saw us right away and were laughing at us. And we didn't even realize!

Anyway, we walked right into their trap. We crept up to a wall, so we could lie behind it and eavesdrop on them. They were talking loudly the whole time—but only to distract us—as we soon realized. Cos that meant we were looking straight ahead all the time and not paying attention to what was behind us.

Which was where the voice came from suddenly: "I wonder what these two little beasts are up to? What d'you reckon, Knuckles?"

"Hm! Spying maybe?" a second voice answered, deeper and hollower than the first.

"Spying?" the first voice answered. "Taking news back to the HJ, huh? They'd better watch out then. We'd have to teach them a few manners, wouldn't we?"

Wow, that gave us a start! We twisted around in shock. Two of them were standing right behind us. They'd crept up on us and had been watching us the whole time—while *we'd been thinking we were watching them. The one who'd spoken first was a brooding type. Shaggy, dark hair, almost black, that fell down in his face. And eyes like coal. With a look that went right through you. I was pretty scared of him. The other was a taller, stronger-looking guy with hands like shovels.*

Before long, the others were there too. They stood in a circle around us, staring, half grinning and half hostile. We sat up with our backs pressed against the wall. I felt sick with fear.

"Hey, I know that one!" someone said, pointing at me. "He came creeping around here once before."

The dark one took a step closer. "Hm, dealt a lousy hand, lads," he said. "Better just admit that the patrols sent you. Then we'll go easy on you."

My heart was in my mouth—I didn't know what to do. Luckily, Tom was braver. He said, "We're not in the HJ. We're done with that crew."

That made them curious. The dark one crouched down in front of us and said, "Let's hear it then, lads. But if you want to get out of this without a bloody nose, it'd better be a damn good story."

So we told them all about it, Morken and the punch-up and the Jungstammführer and that we didn't go to the swearing in, and everything.

Then it went quiet for a bit. Then one of them, lanky, head and shoulders taller than the rest, walked over to the dark one and squatted down beside him.

"What d'you reckon, Flint?" he said.

The dark one looked me in the eyes. I tried to hold his gaze but I couldn't. Eventually I had to look away.

"Not sure," he said. "Could be true. I did hear somewhere about that punch-up. But they could be making it up."

Tom and me, we sat there like we were on trial, waiting for a verdict. But then another voice spoke, higher than the others.

"I know them two," it said. "They're from Klarastrasse."

We turned. A girl! Till then, we hadn't even noticed there were girls there. Or maybe she'd only just arrived. Either way, it was pretty unusual for us. In the HJ, we never had much to do with the BDM, the League of German Girls, and our school class had just been boys too. I think we stared at her open-mouthed.

"Klarastrasse?" the dark one said. "Classy neighbourhood. Got a fair few thrashings from Kriechbaum then, huh?"

We said yes, every week, and then everyone laughed. The tension was gone and I thought: there's a thing—even old Kriechbaum is good for something!

"D'you know them properly?" the dark one asked the girl.

"No. But I reckon they're OK."

"Oh, Tilly! You're just too soft-hearted. You'd tell us half the HJ were OK."

But he must have believed her really, because right away he said to us, "If you're not spies, then what are you up to?"

We looked at each other. Tom didn't say anything. It was my turn.

"We want to join you," I said. I didn't really think. It just burst out.

The dark one thought for a moment. Then he wanted to know everything. Our names, our parents, where we work, etc. We answered the best we could. He stood up and talked to the others, then he came back.

"Sounds all right so far," he said. "But we need to find out a bit more about you. Come again next week. Same day, same time. By the way, what are you still doing down there? Isn't it about time you stood up again?"

We'd been so intimidated we were still sitting with our backs to the wall. Of course, now we jumped up, and everyone laughed at us. But not in a bad way—we had to laugh too. Not long after, we said goodbye and left.

Tom wanted to know why I'd said we wanted to join them. We hadn't said anything about that to each other beforehand. And he was right. I didn't really know what to answer.

Now I've had a chance to think about it. There's something about that lot that I like. They don't keep their voices down when they talk. They look you in the eye and not down at the ground. They muck about and have fun. They wear colourful gear, not the constant brown of the HJ, not like all the grey mice you see in the streets. They seem kind of casual and—free. Yeah, I think that's the right word. They seem free.

Sometimes I wonder what someone like me has to look forward to in life. Always the same mindless work? Just keeping your head down? And then the army, when every day could be your last? There must be something more than that, something special, something worth living for. That's why I said that about joining them. That's what I'll tell Tom tomorrow, when I see him.

23rd May 1941

Beats me how I got through this last week, I've been so edgy. I couldn't concentrate on my work at Ostermann at all and made a pretty big mess of things. And then there were a couple of times when I didn't say "Heil Hitler!" when I needed to go to the bog. So yesterday I got sent to the head of personnel, my best buddy. He'd warned me not to get sent up to him again, and he slapped me about a couple of times. Then he said, next time they'd sack me.

But the others reckoned I shouldn't worry my head about that. "They won't," one of them said. "The worst they'll do is give you a good thrashing and shave your hair off." What a comfort! I think I need to pull my socks up a little way.

This evening, Tom and me went to the Neptune Pool again and met the others. Flint said their enquiries hadn't dug up any dirt. Seemed we were OK. And our story about the HJ checked out. So they'd had a chat and were happy to let us in.

But when we leapt to our feet, he said, "Hang on, hang on! First you've got to pass your initiation test."

"What kind of initiation test?" we asked.

"Oh, it's no big deal. Come with us on our Whitsun trip."

"Where're you going?"

"You'll find out soon enough. Anyway, you're coming. And if you act sensibly," he looked at the others, who turned away and grinned, "then you'll be in. Agreed?"

Course we agreed. We'd go on twenty Whitsun trips if we had to—whatever that meant.

"Great," Flint said. "Just one more thing: we're not taking you in that get-up. You need to be wearing something else when we set off, something a bit sharper, got it?"

First we looked at him and then the others. Wasn't hard to see what he meant. We look like loyal HJ lads who've just taken off their uniforms. But him and the others—they've got style: checked shirts and bright neck scarves, leather jackets and belts with huge buckles. Some have straps on their wrists and kind of fancy hats on their heads. We were almost embarrassed about how we looked.

All the way home we were racking our brains, trying to think how we could get hold of some gear like theirs.

*And what they meant about the initiation. But who cares?
We've done it. We're just happy they'll have us.*

*Flint warned Tom and me. We mustn't write down
anything that could give us or the others away. No names.
No places. Nothing about where we meet or the stuff we
do. He says, if the Nazis search our flats, they mustn't find
anything they could pin on us.*

*Me and Tom talked about it. Seems a bit much. Why
would they search our flats? We're harmless, aren't we? Just
want a bit of freedom. To be left in peace. Not to have to
spend the couple of hours after work on HJ duty too. That's
all. We're not hurting anyone.*

And anyway, so much has happened recently, I've got
*to write it down! Seems like ages since I was a schoolkid
and in the HJ. But it was only weeks ago. It's all going so
fast. It's all flying by and sometimes I'm scared I'll miss it.
I'll forget it. And that it'll stay forgotten if I don't write it
down somewhere.*

*I want something to be left. Always have done. That's
why I always used to write on loose scraps of paper, cos it
was all I had. But they kept getting lost. That's why Mum
gave me this book. On 6th March, my fourteenth birthday.
I can write everything in here. And I do. Flint doesn't
need to know.*

*Course I'm careful. Hiding the book in a safe place.
Even if Flint's right and they come and search the flat and
turn everything upside down, they won't find it.*

No one will find it. Never.

2nd June 1941

*Last week I went with Tom to hunt up some new clothes.
We spent all our wages on them. And yesterday was finally
Whitsun! We'd arranged to meet the others at the station
really early. We were dead excited cos we wanted to see
what they thought of our new get-up.*

*Course they took the piss a bit and we weren't exactly
up to their standards but it was OK. They were satisfied.
Even Flint.*

*"If you don't get a haircut for six months," he said,
"learn a decent song or two and get a few dings from the
HJ, we'll make something of you yet." Seemed like it was
meant as a compliment.*

*We waited till everyone was there, then set off. Took
the train along the Rhine to Bonn, then the tram to
Oberkassel. Then we walked. Into the Siebengebirge mountains. Me and Tom hadn't been there before but the others
seemed to know every last stone. It was steep going till we
got to a view over the whole of Bonn and the Rhine. Then
we came to a lake that the others called the Felsensee. It was
a long way below us, with high rocky cliffs all around. But*

41

there was a path to climb down by, to the only flattish spot on the shore.

When we got down there, we couldn't believe our eyes, Tom and me. In front of us was the lake, so blue among the rocks. And all over the shore were people, dozens of people. People like Flint and the others. People like us?

The moment they spotted us, they rushed over to greet us. Well, mainly Flint and Knuckles and Lanky. They seemed like VIPs there. Me and Tom got some funny looks. We've still got HJ haircuts and a few people made comments. But they got no joy from Flint. He might take the piss a bit but that doesn't mean anyone else can. Any rate, he grabbed one of them by the collar.

"What're you grinning at?" he asked him. "They're with us, see? If you've got any beef with them, come to Knuckles and me."

That was all it took. Nobody wanted to take them two on. After that, they left us in peace.

It was a hot day, plenty of them were in the water already. We'd got sweaty on the way over there, so Flint and Knuckles undressed too and jumped in. Then they waved to us to follow.

We looked round. We didn't have any swimming trunks. And there were some girls on the shore too, looking at us with curiosity.

"Hey, Flint, you bastard!" Tom yelled. "You didn't say to bring trunks!"

"So?" Flint yelled back. "Am I your mother? You two

got to look after yourselves! Get in here! It's part of your initiation!"

We didn't know what to do. The girls started giggling. Then one of our lot came over and helped. The one they called "Goethe", after the poet, cos he's got book learning.

"Do what I do, my friends," he said with a grin. "Strip off and cover your noble manhoods with your hands!"

Then he did exactly that and sidled into the water. Me and Tom took a deep breath and copied him. We were bloody glad to get in. Then, a bit further away, we saw a couple of girls in the water with just as little on as us. Our eyes were on stalks.

Flint had seen them too and he came over. "You'll get used to the sight," he said. "Or maybe you won't. Anyway. C'mon, Knuckles, let's get busy."

He and Knuckles attacked us. We spent the next fifteen minutes with our hands full defending ourselves against the two of them and coming to the surface for air, at least occasionally. But we used to spend a lot of time in the pool, so I think we did quite well.

"Not bad, lads," Flint said, once we were out again and had dried off. "Hope you'll be just as tough later on. When it counts!"

Meanwhile, more and more groups had been arriving. Lots from Cologne, from other parts of town. And some from Düsseldorf and Wuppertal, and even from Essen and Dortmund. But wherever they came from, you could instantly tell they were with us. By their clothes and

43

their hair, which was longer than we were used to. "In the manner of free men" as Goethe said.

Later on, we made a campfire, put potatoes in it and roasted meat over it. Everything was shared. Everyone told the latest stories from their towns. About the patrols, for instance. Their latest dirty tricks and what you could do about them. How to protect yourself against bullying at work. Or the best way to avoid the cops. Everyone had different problems, but they were all kind of similar somehow. Tom and me, most of the time we just sat and listened. Amazed at how many people there were with the same problems as us. You could talk to them for hours!

When it got dark, some of them pulled out guitars and we learnt some of the songs we'd already heard about. Most of them take the mick out of the HJ. One starts: "Big ears, hair shorn, that's how the Hitler Youth are born." Tom and me could hardly keep from laughing. Another one goes: "In a ditch beside the road, lie the Hitler Youth patrol, beaten and sore, they hear us roar, we march away, Edelweiss Pirates, hooray."

That's what everyone down there at the Felsensee called themselves: Edelweiss Pirates. In the evening, around the fire, Flint explained why.

"Pirates are just free people," he said. "They sail here, there and everywhere. Wherever they like. Do what they want. Nobody tells them what to do. And edelweiss grows high up in the mountains. In the wild. Where nobody goes. Nobody can pick it or do anything to harm it. It's just wild and free."

44

Later, when we lay down to sleep, just there, round the fire, I felt what he meant. It was like the world outside with the Nazis and the war and all the rest of the crap had just disappeared. As if we were all there was. Us and the stars up there. And like nobody could touch us. It was exactly what Tom and me had always dreamt of.

It wasn't until this morning, after we woke up, that the world shoved its way in again. We'd just had breakfast and were about to go for another swim. Then a couple of lookouts that had been posted round the lake came and said the HJ were on the march. I asked Flint what they wanted. He reckoned they'd known for ages that we always meet there over Whitsun and now they wanted to really clean us up. He didn't look all that surprised. Must've known from the start they'd be coming.

We ran up the path and saw them miles off. They were coming up the hill in their usual marching formation, always in step. We fanned out and waited for them. High above the lake, on the top of the cliff edge, we met them and it kicked off without much talking.

There were loads of them, more than us at any rate. But we could tell right away that—apart from their leaders, the usual fanatics—their hearts weren't really in it. Course they weren't—someone's dragged them out on their day off and then they're meant to get into a punch-up when they don't even know what it's all about. But we knew damn well. It was about them leaving us in peace for once.

So there was no doubt how it would end. All the same,
Tom and me were scared at first. Noise and shouting
everywhere, everyone really going for it. But at some
point, we spotted Morken and his lot in the crowd. Then
something came over us—we had a score to settle. We went
over to them and then we played our part in the Battle of
Felsensee.

In the end, the HJ boys had to retreat. Their leaders
threatened that next time they'd be back with the SS,
and said our lives wouldn't be worth living from now on
anyway. But we didn't care. We went back down to the lake
and celebrated our victory. The rest of the day was one big
triumph. We felt like we ruled the world!

At some point, Flint took me and Tom aside and
called the other Ehrenfelders over. Some of them had come
off pretty badly and were bleeding, but even that didn't
dampen our mood.

"So, now you've seen what we're about," Flint said.
"D'you still want to join us?"

Did we?! More than ever, we said.

"Then it's all set. You've passed your initiation. From
now on, you're Edelweiss Pirates!"

I don't think Tom and me have ever been prouder of
anything. On the way home, we were almost bursting with
joy.

That was an hour or two ago, it's the middle of the
night now. But I'm too excited to sleep. I'll probably be late
tomorrow and get everything wrong and end up being sent

*to the head of personnel again. But whatever he does to me,
I'll bear it. With a smile.*

*I still can't take in what's happened somehow. I feel like
I've never really lived until now.*

The first thing I noticed was the smell. It was a mix of disinfectant, stale tobacco smoke and the sweetish stench of the kind of ointment that old men rub into their chests to stop themselves coughing. It smelt unpleasant, kind of depressing. My first thought was to about-turn and head off again.

But then I remembered how much effort it had been to get there in the first place. I hadn't been able to get the old man I'd met at the cemetery out of my head. I'd gone down there several times over the next few days but I hadn't seen him. I was afraid I'd scared him off with my questions.

After waiting in vain a third time, I went to ask the cemetery caretaker about the old man. I thought if I told the caretaker his brother's name, and where he was buried, perhaps he could help me. I was in luck—the caretaker knew the old man, because he sometimes put flowers on his brother's grave on his behalf. So I discovered that the man's name was "Josef Gerlach" and that he lived near the cemetery, in a kind of home for single old men. And that was where I was now standing, in the entrance hall, trying to get used to the strange smell.

A man sitting in a glass box waved me over. "Who do you want to see?" he asked.

"Mr Gerlach."

"Josef Gerlach?"

"Yes."

He pointed across to the far corner of the lobby. "Take the lift over there. Third floor, apartment 309. And keep quiet—it's afternoon-nap time!"

I did as he said. A couple of elderly people were just getting into the lift. I didn't want to get in with them so I waited at the bottom. The house rules were displayed on the wall. Black letters on a red background, three closely-printed columns. What on earth am I doing here? I wondered.

I'd thought about that on the way there too. I'd thought about my grandfather. Especially the last time we saw each other, before he died so suddenly and unexpectedly. There'd been several times when he started telling me a story. A story from his childhood that seemed to mean a lot to him. But I'd had my mind on my own problems and hadn't been that interested in hearing it. Next time, I'd said. And then there hadn't been a next time.

Whenever I thought of it, I felt really bad. He'd wanted to tell *me*, and maybe nobody else. Because it had been important to him that I knew about it. And I hadn't listened. That was probably the reason I went to his grave— and probably also the reason I was here now, visiting this old man. Because at the cemetery, when he invited me, I'd seen the same expression in his eyes as in Grandad's when he'd wanted to tell his story. That must be it: you don't often get the chance to make up for something.

I had to wait a long time for the lift. It was slow and took for ever on each floor. When I got out on the third floor, there was nobody in sight. I walked down the corridor, looking for the right room. It was kind of oppressive although I couldn't have said why. The carpet, the wallpaper, the pictures on the walls: they were all tasteful and went well together. But perhaps that was it. They were trying to make it *seem* nice because it wasn't *actually* nice.

Eventually I found room number 309. I stood outside it for some time, not daring to knock. What would I say to the old man? Maybe I'd come at a bad time and everything would be silly and embarrassing. Maybe he'd have forgotten me and wouldn't even know who I was.

But then I knocked. It was quite a while before anything happened. First the door opened just a crack, but then it was opened wide. The old man was standing in front of me. He looked at me in astonishment, then he smiled.

"Come in," he said. I think he was pleased about my visit.

22nd June 1941

*It was the first thing we heard when we got back from our
weekend trip today: the war against Russia's started. Some
people had been expecting it for ages, but we had never
wanted to believe it'd actually happen. So the news was a
real shock.*

*We haven't really felt much of the war yet. When it
kicked off two years ago, everyone was scared and didn't
know what'd happen. But then hardly anything changed.
Except you could only get food with a ration card. But so
long as you're not daft, you can get by OK on the rations.
And you're not allowed to listen to foreign radio stations—
that makes you a "radio criminal". But loads of people
do. Secretly, when the block warden's not around. "Radio
Nippes" they call the BBC round our way as a joke cos
Nippes used to be so far out of Cologne it was like a foreign
country.*

*And there's the blackout. Everyone has these black
blinds on their windows and you have to pull them down
when it gets dark. There's trouble if you forget. And massive trouble if you forget again. Could be a saboteur, trying
to attract enemy aircraft. That's why there are no lights
outside in the evenings. Street lamps and shop windows are
dark, even cars have to have caps on their headlights.*

But none of that is really bad. We haven't seen anyone get killed or injured. That's all at the front. And that's a long way off, somewhere over the hills and far away. Nobody talks about it much. All you hear are victory reports on the radio. And you can buy little booklets at the kiosk about the heroic deeds of German soldiers. Like the cowboy stories in the old days.

But now things won't be so quiet, say some of the older men. Russia's not Poland. And not France either. The country's too big, we can't beat them. And we need to watch out or it'll backfire on us. Stupid to pick a fight with everyone at once. Course they only whisper it. And only if there're no strangers around.

We spent awhile just sitting together this evening. Flint and Knuckles were there, Goethe and Lanky, Tilly and Floss, her friend. And Tom and me of course. The fun of our trip was over. Cos one thing's for certain now: this war's going to go on and on. And who knows what ideas them at the top will come up with next. What they might do to people like us!

9th July 1941

Actually, it's best not to worry too much. It's summer and who knows how many summers we've got left. We're just happy, Tom and me, that we've found the others and they let us join in. We meet up with them nearly every evening.

Always outdoors, of course. We get enough dusty air at work and there's not enough room at home. We have to get out, even though it's illegal. Or rather precisely because it is!

For a long time, we met at the Neptune and treated the place like we were alone in the world. Didn't waste a thought on the patrols. Figured we were shot of them, after Flint and the others chucked them out of Ehrenfeld back then.

"It was their own fault," Flint told Tom and me once. "Wouldn't leave us alone. Kept asking to see our papers. Started pushing us around and all that. One evening they went too far. Had to show us what they'd got. So then it was only fair if we defended ourselves, wasn't it?"

So there, we thought—we know Flint's idea of self-defence! Any rate, for ages we felt safe and weren't on the lookout for trouble. So we were dead surprised when the patrol turned up again two weeks ago. Probably cos of the business at the Felsensee.

It was late, dark already, we were about to go. Suddenly there they were. All much older than us and easily twice as many of them. It was just as well they had their hefty boots on. It makes them look impressive when they stamp about the streets in them. But you can hear them two kilometres upwind.

We didn't hesitate, just scrammed. Scattered, so they'd have to decide who to chase first. Most of them followed Flint and Knuckles cos they've got a bone to pick with them. But Tom and me had some on our heels too. We kept ducking down side streets and we know every cut-through in our neck of the woods, so eventually we shook them off.

Fortunately, they didn't get any of the others either— not even Goethe and he's the slowest. But it was a close thing and we've decided we'd better not meet at the pool any more. They know the square too well now. And it's too open, there's nowhere to hide. So now we prefer to meet in a park. There's the Stadtgarten on Venloer Wall if we want to stay round here, or we can go straight to the Volksgarten.

That's our new favourite. There are hundreds of hidden corners between the bushes, with benches and flower beds and everything you get in a park like that. Most days, there are groups from other parts of town there too—each with their own patch. We post lookouts at the entrances. If they see a patrol or the police, they jump on a bike and warn us. Then we scarper, wait till the coast's clear and go back later on.

We feel safe in the Volksgarten. It's our own little Reich. The patrols haven't got the brains to catch us there. By the time they show up, we're long gone. And when they've gone, we're back again. That's how it goes. These days, we're almost sad if they don't come. Like there's something missing.

It's so much fun. Like a game. I wish this summer could last for ever!

We're a real close gang these days. There are ten of us, and today we decided that's enough for the time being. The more of us there are, the greater the danger that someone will spill the beans. Or that some other stupid thing will happen.

We're trying to be the exact opposite of the HJ. That's why we don't have a leader. Nobody gives orders, nobody has to obey. But Flint is a bit special. Kind of like our captain. That's where he gets his name: Captain Flint from Treasure Island. *There's something a bit sinister about him. Which is why I was properly scared of him at first. But not any more. Now I admire him. Because he won't be told. Always does what he thinks is right. Always knows what to do. I wish I was like that.*

I don't know everyone's real names, not even Flint's. We only use our pirate names with each other. Real names don't matter, they're from another life. Besides, this way it doesn't matter if anyone overhears us—they still won't know who we are.

Flint's best friend is Knuckles. I like him but I've hardly ever spoken to him. He doesn't say much at all, but he's built like a bear. He was a fortress in the battle at the Felsensee. He scrapes by as a labourer. Tilly says he was in a home cos his parents died young. She says Flint once got him out of a jam and now Knuckles loves him like a brother. She doesn't know what it was, they don't talk about it. But

55

one thing's for sure: if anyone gets after Flint, they'll have Knuckles to deal with. And vice versa.

After Flint, the most important of us is Lanky. He knows most about the Nazis and everything to do with them. His father was a communist, and so are his whole family. Most of them aren't around, they got nicked. But he learnt a lot from them. If me or Tom want to know anything political, we ask him. He's only a year older than us, like Flint and Knuckles, but he knows so much. Seems totally grown-up. No idea why. Maybe because he's so tall. But it's not just that. There's something else.

Goethe's a special case. He's too posh to be one of us really, cos his dad's a teacher and they've got their own house and all that. But apparently, he had a crush on a girl in the group once, before me and Tom were around, and even though she's been gone for ages, the others decided he could stay. Cos he can play the guitar so well and knows so many songs, Flint said once. And that's true: no one can beat him there. When Goethe's around, even our racket sounds halfway decent. He reckons it's almost impossible to keep peasants like us in tune, but he lives in hope. He's no use in fights with the HJ—he's too weedy. So he looks after the instruments.

Then there's Ferret. He's the only one a month or two younger than me and Tom. He got his name cos he's so small and pointy-faced. His family's even poorer than the rest of us and that's saying something. I went round to his once, a couple of weeks ago. He lives with his mum and brothers and sisters in a real dump. But the thing I like about him is: he doesn't let it get him down. Never lets anything get him down. Just the opposite: if we're in a mood, it's usually him who cheers us up. Strange. I wonder where he finds the strength.

Tilly was the first of the girls we met. When she helped us out, back at the Neptune Pool. She's from Philippstrasse. I remember me and Tom playing with her a few times when we were kids. But then we lost track of her. She does some kind of sewing work here in Ehrenfeld, making winter uniforms for the army. I don't think her mum's all that keen on her hanging around with us. But she doesn't say she can't. Wouldn't do any good anyway, knowing Tilly. She doesn't take orders from anyone.

Her best friend is Floss. They go to the Workers' Swimming Club together, down at the pool. She's the only one who can keep up with Lanky in debates. Her family aren't commies but socialists. But there aren't many of them left either. She lives with her mum and two little brothers, who she looks after. I like her and Tom likes her more. She's cheeky and you need to watch out for her mouth. I think she's the only one of us that even Flint respects.

And then there's Maja. I don't know much about her. Just that she lives with her grandparents and works on a production line in some canning factory. No idea who her parents were or what happened to them. She doesn't talk about it. Doesn't say much at all, she's pretty shy. Maybe because she's got this cleft lip. But she likes music, I know *that much. Likes it when Goethe plays something on the guitar and then she plays it after him. But otherwise she's usually quiet. Like there's something inside her that she can't talk about. Like there's something nobody must find out about.*

Anyway, that's them: our new friends. Nowadays we're just there, Tom and me, like that's how it's always been, and we've lost our names too. For Tom it was easy. His real name's Karl. Karl Gescher. But since we started school, everyone's called him Tom cos he looks like the boy in the illustrations for Tom Sawyer. The others reckoned the name was OK, he could keep it.

And me? They call me Gerlo. Not very exciting, but nobody could think of anything better. I'm not a captain like Flint, not as strong as Knuckles or as tall as Lanky. An average name for an average lad. But I'm one of them. And that's all that matters.

3rd August 1941

Today I realized something odd. None of us has a dad any more. Well, almost none of us. I wonder if that's just chance. Or if there's more to it.

Some of them lost their fathers a long time ago. Tom, for instance. I can hardly remember it—we were only little. The Nazis had just come to power, marched through Ehrenfeld with their clomping boots. In Berlin, the Reichstag was on fire, and then the dads of a couple of boys on our street disappeared. Tom's too. I was with him the last time his dad came back. He told us about a camp called Börgermoor, and then suddenly he sang us a song. His voice was all shaky. It was about peat-bog soldiers who marched into the moor with spades, but really only wanted to go home to their families. By the end, he had tears in his eyes. The next day, he had to go again. He never came back.

I had my dad a few years longer. Till the war. They drafted him right when it started, he had to go to Poland. Every week there was a field postcard from him. He wrote that he was fine and he'd be back with us soon. Always the same. He never told us what was really happening. When the campaign was over, he had to stay in Poland. Even when the war against France broke out last year.

That was the time when everyone was scared. France! Hope it won't be like the last war, we all thought. But then there were reports of one victory after another. Within a few weeks, it was over: Paris occupied, France finished. People celebrated in the streets. It was 22nd June. The same day that Mum and me learnt that Dad had fallen in Poland. Fighting rebels. We sat there with his field postcards and could hear the crowds cheering outside. It was like the whole world was laughing at us.

These days I know that we're not the only ones. Floss and Lanky are like Tom—their dads disappeared early on. Tilly and Ferret are like me: theirs were killed in the

*war. Flint, Knuckles and Maja I don't know about, either
way, their dads aren't around. The only one who still has
a father is Goethe. But there are lots of ways he's different
from us.*

*The patrols like to call us an "unpatriotic rabble with
no fatherland". Until now that either made me laugh or
made me cross, depending on my mood. But I've realized
they're not that wrong. Not completely. A "rabble with no
fathers"—that's us!*

19th August 1941

*Recently, the patrols have changed tactics. Seems they've
caught on. They start by crashing through the Volksgarten
to flush us out. Then they vanish again—but that's just
the start. As soon as we're back and feel safe, they set the
police on us. A couple of times, they crept up on us through
the bushes and took us by surprise. And that can be pretty
dangerous cos they're armed and generally in a mighty bad
temper.*

*Mind you, we've adjusted too now and know what
to do. First, it's important to know what kind of policeman you're dealing with. There are two sorts: the proper
Nazis and the not-so-proper Nazis. If it's the second sort,
everything's fine. They usually take a fatherly approach
and try to talk sense into us. Then we act all downcast.
Promise to go home straight away, never, never to hang*

around anywhere after dark and definitely never, never to do anything wrong again for the rest of our lives. They usually let us go and we head straight to the next-nearest park.

But if it's the first sort, the strict ones, we have to think of something else. They always want to see our papers and if we don't show them—which we can't, cos we've never got them with us—they get tricky. Fortunately, we've got our secret weapons: Ferret, Flint and Floss. You can't beat them when it comes to the police.

It happened again yesterday evening. We were in the Volksgarten, messing around and joking with the girls. The patrol had been round and gone off again, so we thought that'd be it. Goethe had his guitar and we'd started singing. One of our favourite songs: "We were sat in Johnny's old dive bar, playing cards and drinking schnapps, Jim Baker, that no-good varmint, and Jo, the Japanese chap." But just as we were giving it full welly, there was suddenly a cop in front of us. He must have crept up on us, we were totally caught out. And we could see at once: this was a real tough nut!

He started bellowing at us right away. What were we thinking of, hanging around here in the middle of the night, making such a din? Didn't we know it was forbidden? And where were our papers, if we pleased?

First we tried the usual lines:

"Papers? What papers?"

"Forbidden? Since when?"

"Surely you don't mean us?"

But that wasn't going to fly with this one. He gave us a dirty look, then targeted Ferret. They usually go for him cos he's so ugly and they reckon they can do what they like with him.

"Hey, you! Come here, you little rat!"

Ferret leapt up like he'd been bitten by a tarantula.

"Certainly, Sergeant, sir!"

Course the bloke wasn't a Sergeant, just a plain, ordinary constable. But we always do that with the police. Partly to make fun of them. And partly cos some of them actually feel flattered by it. Some of them. Not this one, of course.

"What are you lot up to here?" he thundered.

Ferret clicked his heels together. "We're busy, sir, sergeant, sir!"

"Busy, huh? Well, I'm longing to hear what a lousy mob like you might be busy with. Out with it!"

"Permission to speak, sir: dreaming of the final victory and lost track of time!"

There were a few seconds of total silence. We were all holding our breath. I don't know how Ferret does it, but he sounds dead serious when he says stuff like that. Like it's straight from the heart. Even the cop was unsure for a moment. But then he loomed over him.

"Now you pay attention, my lad! Don't get cheeky with me! It wouldn't take us long to deal with your type, got that?"

"Definitely, sergeant, sir!" Ferret clicked his heels together again, this time so loudly it made your ears throb. "Wouldn't take long to deal with my type. Thank you for the advice, sergeant, sir!"

Meanwhile, the rest of us had made a circle round them.

"Come on, leave him alone," Tom said from one side. "Can't you see that he's all in a muddle? He's talking gibberish!"

"I'll make gibberish of you," growled the constable. Then he looked from one of us to the next. Finally, he stopped at Flint.

"You there!" he said, pointing his finger at him. "Are you the ringleader here?"

That happens every time. No matter what Flint does, eventually they single him out. You can just see that there's something special about him. Luckily, he's got a good way of dealing with it: he starts stammering and acts like a complete idiot. Which he did yesterday too.

"W-what? Me? C-c-const..."

Tom dug him in the ribs. "Hey, he's a sergeant!" he whispered.

Flint stared at him for a few seconds like he needed to think about that. Then he turned back to the policeman. "S-s-sarge..."

We could hardly stop ourselves laughing. The policeman was the only person who wasn't amused. He started shouting again. We should now kindly show him our papers! His hand went to his belt. Where his gun was.

63

*High time for Floss to make her entrance! She was
standing behind him so he couldn't see her, while Tilly and
Maja had slipped away into the bushes a long time before.*

"This is all my fault, sergeant," she said.

*He turned round. Hadn't been expecting a girl's voice,
apparently. "What do you mean, your fault? What are you
doing here at all? Aren't you ashamed to be in the park in
the middle of the night with this rabble? Does your mother
know where you are?"*

*"That's just it. My mother is ill. I need to get medicine
for her. And these boys are walking with me. To makes sure
nothing happens to me."*

*She gave him such a pathetic look. That was the signal.
We all started talking at him from all sides. Whatever
came into our heads:*

*"Yes, that's right. We're just walking with her. And
you'd arrest us for that!"*

*"Imagine if she got attacked and her mum didn't get
her medicine!"*

"Exactly! Do you want the blame if she dies?"

"We'll complain to your superiors!"

*"It's a scandal, the way you get treated here! They
ought to put it in the papers!"*

*"Years as a doormat in the Hitler Youth and now
this!"*

"Is this what you mean by national community?"

*We babbled on at him without pausing for breath for
several minutes till he didn't know whether he was coming*

or going. Then, at a nod from Flint, we scattered, leapt on our bikes and off we went. The poor fellow was so muddled he didn't even think to grab at least one of us.

At work today I caught myself laughing about it a couple of times. But then again, we shouldn't push our luck too far. They won't take it for ever. What if a whole troop of them come next time? Don't waste time talking, but just reach for their guns and collar the lot of us? Then our cover'd be blown. They'd know who we are, where we live and where we work.

Yes! Maybe we ought to be more careful. I'll have to talk to the others.

4th September 1941

Horst's written from Sonthofen. Complaining that he couldn't make head or tail of my last letter. That it was full of nonsense. Which is true of course. I still didn't feel up to telling him that I'm done with the HJ. So I just wrote a load of stupid blah-blah.

To be honest, I'm scared of him finding out. Because I know how disappointed he'll be. And somehow, I still care most about what he thinks. Well, after Tom and Flint of course.

He's been down in Bavaria for four years now. I remember it all so clearly. Found myself thinking about it when I read his letter today. Someone from the HJ came to my parents—a real high-up. He told them about the Adolf Hitler Schools they were setting up. That only the very best would be sent there. The "elite of the future Reich". And that Horst had been chosen.

My parents didn't know what to think at first. Our Horst at an elite school? But it seemed that your background didn't make a difference there. Horst's a real sporting ace. And besides, he looks the perfect Nazi image of a true Aryan: blond, wiry and with steel-blue eyes. Like the boys in the posters. So they were desperate to have him.

If he does well at this school, every door will be open to him, the bloke from the HJ said. Every career in the state and the Party, right up to the top. Which meant that Horst would be the very first in our family to have a chance to do something other than break his back shifting in gloomy factories. When my parents heard that, they had no choice: they agreed—even though they didn't normally have much time for the Nazis. And so Horst went to the Ordensburg Sonthofen. In spring '37. At the same time that Tom and me started in the HJ.

Since then, I've seen him precisely one week per year. He's not allowed home more often and we're totally banned from visiting him. They're dead strict about that.

I remember him coming home for a visit after his first year. I'd just done my Pimpfenprobe, the test so I could join the Jungvolk, and I thought I was really grown-up. But almost the moment Horst got off the train in the station, I felt dead puny again. He looked so good in his uniform, so tall and strong. "Squirt" he called me. But he wasn't trying to put me down. He was happy to see me again.

But he was pretty cool towards our parents. He didn't want Mum to hug him. And he practically ignored Dad. You could feel so clearly that he wasn't prepared to listen to him any more. Felt superior to him. It confused me at first. But then I was fascinated.

In the evenings, when the oldies were asleep, we were able to sit together again and finally talk about everything without anyone listening—just like the old days. Horst was dead proud of me. Cos I'd passed the test. I had to tell him everything, down to the tiniest detail. Our parents hadn't been that interested. But Horst was different. He was as pleased as if it had been him doing the test.

"That's the way, squirt," he said, and boxed me on the shoulder. "I'm counting on you. Things have changed, you know. Today we can do anything. Whatever we want. Don't let anyone tell you any different. Not even the old man. He hasn't got a clue."

There was something conspiratorial about the way he said that. I liked it. He'd really changed. Something had happened to him at that school.

I budged up closer to him. "Tell me about Sonthofen! What's it like?"

"Oh boy, listen up!" He laughed and shook his head. "I knew it'd be rough there, but I didn't have a clue…"

And then he talked. About how they had to walk through ice and snow in the winter, barefoot and bare chested. How they had to jump into the swimming pool from the ten-metre diving board, with full kit, packs and steel helmets. How they had to bear pain and hardship beyond anything anyone knew existed. And how, if anyone showed the slightest weakness, they'd immediately all be punished.

"Didn't you ever want to leave?" I asked. "To come home?"

"Course I did, at first. Thought I'd never make it. And I wouldn't have done alone. But I made friends. And you don't want to embarrass yourself in front of them. It makes you strong. Like with real comrades, you know."

We had a real long talk that evening. And the days after that. Till he left again. I admired and envied him. For everything he'd experienced and the stories he could tell. About his time at the Ordensburg. About all the tests of courage and the amazing comradeship. About the hard training that only the best could manage. It's strange: I was eleven then and he was thirteen. But it seemed like there was a whole lifetime between us.

Back then, I swore never to disappoint him. "I'm counting on you," he'd said. And he was right to! I wanted to be like him. I was dead set on it.

But then the war came and all the playing at soldiers in the HJ, Morken and everything that's happened this year. I'm not sad about it, no way. I'm glad not to have *anything more to do with the HJ and that Tom and me are Edelweiss Pirates now. It's just that when a letter from Horst comes, it makes me think. Cos I've broken my oath. What will he say when I have to fess up to him?*

28th September 1941

Last night's mission was a total success. The whole neighbourhood's laughing about it now. But nobody knows that it was us. And let's hope it stays that way, thank you very much. Cos if it came out, we really would be in trouble.

We had the idea a few days ago. We were in the Volksgarten talking about all kinds of stuff that popped into our heads. I don't remember who started it, but somehow, we got talking about the Block Wardens. They hassle everyone now, cos they've got so much power while the war's on. In the old days, they just used to collect fees from people in the Party and distribute the Völkischer Beobachter *newspaper. But these days they're real pests. Always sniffing around to check that everyone's blacking out properly and that nobody's listening to the British radio or anything else that's banned. All decent people hate them.*

It's really bad round Tom's way. He reckons his block warden—Kuhlmann, his name is—is worse than a prison warden. He's denounced people and handed them over to the Gestapo. Whether they did anything or not. Just cos he's got a bone to pick with them. Tom says he creeps round after dark every evening, going from one window to the next. Tries to peer through the cracks in the blinds. And if he notices anything, he turns up on people's doorsteps the next day threatening them. Says they've got to do this and that for him or he'll report them.

Lanky said, we ought to teach someone like that a lesson. One he wouldn't forget in a hurry. We came up with all kinds of ideas of things we could do to him. Just for fun. But at some point, Flint said, "Why stop at talk, people? Let's actually go through with something for once!"

So last night was it. Tom said Kuhlmann takes the same route on his rounds every evening and always at the same time. We thought that level of German order and thoroughness needs punishing! And Ferret had the bright idea of how to do it.

Yesterday evening, when it got dark, we met at Tom's block. There's a place where the ground floor windows over the inner yard are a bit higher so you can't look in through them directly. But Kuhlmann doesn't let that stop him, Tom said. He just jumps up and pulls himself up on the windowsill so he can carry on spying.

That's the spot we chose. Went up to the windows. All the blinds were down so nobody saw us. Ferret got on Knuckles's shoulders and brushed a windowsill with glue. Then we hid opposite and waited. Wasn't long before Kuhlmann turned up. Like Tom said: from window to window, pressing his nose up against them all. Revolting.

Eventually he got to the window we'd prepared. We held our breath. And yep, he jumped up, held onto the sill and pulled himself up. We could hear him panting across the yard. When he'd snooped enough, he wanted to let go and jump down. But he couldn't, his fingers were set fast as cement. Ferret got hold of some damn good glue.

It was a sight for sore eyes. He kicked his legs and tried to get at least one hand free. But that was a no go. Then he spent a couple of minutes hanging there motionless. Probably racking his brains about how to get out of there without embarrassing himself. But apparently he couldn't think of anything, cos eventually he started calling for help. Really quietly at first, so the whole block wouldn't hear. But nobody ever got anywhere by calling for help quietly. So he got louder and louder. Must have started to panic too.

We were crouched down in our hiding place, making sure we didn't laugh. Couldn't have him knowing who to blame for the mess. Then one of the blinds went up, right above us. A man looked out.

"C'mere!" he called over his shoulder to someone indoors, after a while staring at Kuhlmann.

We could hear his wife's voice behind him:

"Why? Wassup?"

"C'mere now! That pig's 'angin' from the winder!"

His wife had come closer. "Wot d'ya mean? Wot pig?"

She came to stand beside him. They both looked out. We could hear her laughing.

"Serves the bastard right," the man said.

Kuhlmann called for help again.

"C'mon, leave 'im 'angin'," the wife said, going away from the window. "An' shut that fing again!"

The next moment, the blind slammed down again. I had bellyache with holding back so much laughter. The others were the same. We were rolled up in our hideout.

Then more windows opened. Wasn't much sympathy for Kuhlmann. No way. People hate types like him. They mightn't dare do anything about them but they won't help if they're in a jam. They'll have a long wait.

Eventually, some people did take pity on him. Probably Party members—there are some of those here too, of course. Soon, half the yard was full of onlookers. It was getting a bit too hot for comfort. So we waited for a good moment and scrammed.

Today, Tom told us what happened next. They tried everything to get Kuhlmann down from there but nothing helped. In the end, they had to tip boiling water over his hands, and he finally got free. But, Tom says, his fingertips will be stuck to that windowsill for ever.

Flint reckons that was just the job for a Saturday evening for him, and we ought to do something like that again. And why not? So long as only pigs like Kuhlmann get hurt, it's no big problem. They're just getting what's coming to them. Aren't they?

26th October 1941

Last night they took the Rosenfelds away. The old people
from upstairs. Because they're Jewish. The noise woke us up,
Mum and me. We went out onto the stairs to see what was
going on. There were some Gestapo who chased us away.
Nothing to see, they said. Told us not to concern ourselves
with things that were none of our business. My mum was
white as chalk. She's afraid of those Gestapo types.

Presumably the Rosenfelds are now on one of those
Jewish trains that keep going out of Deutz station. To
the east. Apparently they go into old people's homes there.
Where it's just them and their kind. And they're not in so
much danger as here.

Anyway, I couldn't sleep last night. Got up and sat on
the windowsill. All kinds of stuff in my head. I looked over
to Venloer Strasse, and suddenly remembered the thing
with Mr Goldstein. That was only just down the road. I
hadn't thought about it for ages, but the business with the
Rosenfelds made me remember.

It was three years ago, on the Night of Broken Glass,
as they call it now. I was eleven and I remember lying in
bed when the noise kicked off out there. In the middle of
the night. I ran out even though Dad yelled at me to stay
here. The noise was loudest on Venloer Strasse, so I ran
that way. And I saw what was happening. There were
Nazi Brownshirts everywhere, smashing the windows of the
Jewish shops. Others ran up into the flats, pulled the Jews

out into the road and beat them up. You could hear the women screaming upstairs.

At first I was so confused, I couldn't think clearly at all. But then I thought of Mr Goldstein. He had a little kiosk down the road. I often stood there with Tom but we never had the money to buy anything. So he used to slip us something now and then. Little sweets and stuff. We liked him. And: he was a Jew!

I ran that way. His kiosk was bashed in too. His stuff was lying in the road, the Brownshirts had trampled it with their boots. But the worst thing was Mr Goldstein himself. He was crawling around among his things, trying to save what he could. The Brownshirts yelled at him to stop but he didn't. So they kicked him. He collapsed but then he hauled himself up. He went to pick something up from the ground—right in front of one of the Brownshirts. And he kicked him right in the face.

I remember running over to him. But not whether I said anything. He was lying on his back, staring at me. I'm not sure if he recognized me. His face was covered in blood. And then he suddenly held out the thing he'd picked up to me. It was a little music box. I took it, but before I could do anything else, the Brownshirt grabbed me by the collar and gave me a shove that sent me halfway across the street.

I don't know what happened after that. Only that Mr Goldstein disappeared. I never saw him again. But I've still got his music box. It's in the drawer. I kept it cos it reminds me of him. I never found out why he wanted *to rescue that of all things. Maybe it was a gift. Or an heirloom or something.*

Anyway, I found myself thinking of all that again as I sat on the windowsill looking out. I wondered if Mr Goldstein was in one of those old folks' homes. But when I was with the others today, I asked Lanky about it. He just laughed and said I shouldn't believe cock and bull stories like that. There might be all kinds of stuff in the east, but definitely no old people's homes. Probably, the Jews have to slave away until they're done in. And then... He shrugged and we talked about something else.

I think it's a pity the Rosenfelds aren't there any more. Who knows who'll move in now? Probably some spy, Flint said. Says they often do that. So I need to be damn careful for the next little while.

But he didn't have to tell me that. I've worked that out for myself by now.

The old man's flat was small. It seemed to consist only of a single room. Later, when I spent more time there, I discovered that there was also a bathroom, a tiny kitchen and a balcony, but on that day, I only saw that one room and the few things it contained. A table with a couple of chairs, a bed, a chest of drawers, a wardrobe and two canaries in a cage on the windowsill: that was all. I noticed a strange object on top of the drawers, something lying in a velvet-lined box. I wasn't sure, but it looked like an old music box.

The furniture looked cheap, as if it had been bought in a closing-down sale. I found myself thinking about how my parents and I live. We've got a house on the edge of town. I can't exactly claim that I'm always happy with it but—at least it's a house. Compared to this! The idea that the chest of drawers and wardrobe might contain everything the old man owned was depressing. Is this all you get left with after such a long life? I couldn't help wondering.

I turned to face him. He'd shut the door now but was still standing with his hand on the latch. He didn't seem to know what to say. I couldn't think of anything either.

"You—you haven't been to see your brother again," I eventually tried to make a start.

"No. That hasn't been possible in the last few days." He let go of the latch and pointed at his bed. "I was ill. This is the first day I've been back on my feet."

He did look very pale. I found myself thinking about him lying in this little room for days, in the bed beside his chest of drawers and wardrobe, not able to go out. It was a sad image.

"How did you find me?" he asked.

I told him the story of the cemetery caretaker. He seemed to be pleased that I'd put so much effort into the search. After listening to everything, he walked to the table and waved me over.

"Would you like a drink of cocoa—now you're here?"

I declined hastily. "No, no thank you. I can't stay long."

He smiled. "But you surely didn't come just to say hello and then vanish again? Well, come and sit down, at least."

We sat at the table. It was right next to a small window, through which you could see out into the home's garden. It was very quiet. Too quiet for my taste.

"I don't even know your name," said the old man, once he'd fetched two cups and put them on the table.

"Daniel. Like my grandad."

"Daniel?" The name seemed to move him in some way—or remind him of something. He looked out of the window for quite a while, then he ran his hand over his eyes.

"You told me about your story, and that it might interest me," I said, when his silence had gone on too long. "That's why I came. I'd like to hear it."

He looked at me, and it felt as if he'd been somewhere else entirely and first had to find his way back into his little room. Then he stood up, walked over to the chest of drawers, pulled out a book and handed it to me.

"This is my story," he said.

I took the book and opened it. It was very old; I could see that at a glance. The pages were covered in handwriting that looked almost painted on—as if it belonged to someone who didn't write often and so was making an extra effort. The pages were yellowish, there were water stains on a lot of them, some were ripped at the edges but very carefully stuck back together.

"When did you write all this?" I asked, after I'd leafed through it for a while.

"Oh, an eternity ago. That's what I used to feel, anyway. But now it doesn't seem so long, it seems to have come closer again. Strange, huh?"

I went to hand the book back but he declined.

"No, no, keep it. It's for you."

"You want to just give it to me?"

"You'll look after it. I know that."

I opened the book again and let the pages run through my fingers.

"Why are you giving it to me in particular?"

"Oh, just read it," he said, looking out of the window again. "Then you'll understand."

17th March 1942

It's starting to feel like spring outside. I'll be glad when winter's over. Coal's been damn hard to get recently and it's no fun always sitting around in the icy cold. And I'll be able to meet the others more often again once the evenings get longer. That's why this diary's coming out of hibernation too. There hasn't been much to write about for months. Just a matter of scraping through somehow. But I get the feeling we're in for more interesting times now.

Specially cos we're going to be able to go on trips again. Although we'll have to be more careful this year than last. The HJ have come up with a new wheeze: "youth war deployment". Any job where there aren't enough men cos there're all at the front is now HJ business. They've got to help the fire brigade and with the post. Give out ration cards, run errands and work on phone switchboards. Help with the harvest. And collect everything you can think of: scrap metal, windfall fruit, herbs—anything that still has any kind of value.

So now they're trying to force us back into service again. At work, there're all kinds of bullying for apprentices who aren't in the HJ. We get lumped with the worst drudge jobs. Hours scrubbing the factory hall or doing

79

other stuff that's so mindless it makes you sick in the head. And we get thrashings too, of course. "Skivers" they call us. Wow, I hate that word now! And we have to put in an appearance in front of the factory boss every day or two. Then he tells us he's never been as ashamed of anyone as he is of us scum who don't even know when it's time to do their duty and play their part. And that in his eyes, we're spongers, stabbing our own people in the back.

Sometimes it's hard to stand it. But at least I've got the others now. When we meet up, each of us can let off steam. We swear till we're blue in the face. And then we cheer each other up again.

Although I've been thinking a bit recently. About being called "skivers" and that. I was wondering if there was anything in it. Cos some of the stuff the HJ do isn't that bad. For instance, they collect woollen blankets and give them to old folks to stop them freezing in the winter. And the BDM girls help in the kindergartens and old people's homes. And what are we doing?

Today I talked to the others about it. But they gave me a proper ticking off. Specially Lanky.

"Don't let 'em bring you to heel, Gerlo," he said. "This whole war is just one big pile of shit. Every day, thousands of poor sods are dying out there. Cos they set them on each other without even asking if they wanted to fight. And why? So that one day the Greater German Reich can be a Gigantic German Reich! That's all! Anyone who joins in is an idiot—whether they're at the front or here at home."

"Yeah, that's right," Floss said. "Why d'you think the BDM girls are going into the kindergartens now? So the women who work there can work in the arms factories. Where they can make even more grenades and even more bullets, so that the boys at the front can shoot each other's heads off even better. You really don't need to feel guilty, Gerlo. Just don't join in, it's the best we can do."

The others agreed. Even Flint. At some point he stood up and came over to me.

"D'you know who the real skiver is, Gerlo?"

"No. Who?"

"Ha, that fine Mr Factory Boss. Is he out on the front? Is he collecting blankets? Working in a children's home? Course not! An' he never will. All he's doing is making a mint of money from the war. He's the one stabbing his people in the back, man, not you. Remember that the next time he's standing over you!"

That really opened my eyes, the way he said that. Bloody hell, he's right, I thought. And so are the others!

"But—if we mean this," I said, "shouldn't we stop work altogether? In the end it's all for the war!"

"We've got to have something to live on," Flint said. "Best copy Knuckles and me. Do the bare minimum! Just enough so they don't sack you. And if—by complete accident—something gets dropped and broken now and then, that's no bad thing. Just make sure no one notices it was you. Got it?"

I spent a long time thinking about that. Not about if we're doing the right thing, I've got no doubts about *that any more. No, I was wondering what I can do at Ostermann to really put one over on the boss. Flint and Knuckles are right. And I'll try to do the same from tomorrow too.*

14th April 1942

Since the HJ have been on war deployment, the patrols have the upper hand again. They've probably been ordered to drive us off the street and out of the parks once and for all and, while they're at it, to intimidate us into doing our duties again. And they're taking it damn seriously. The patrols are now officially the junior SS. So they want to show that they're real hard nuts.

They're armed with truncheons now, and ever since they got them they've been feeling mighty powerful. Always playing around with them and slapping them into their palms so that everyone gets the message not to fool with them. Anyway, at first we weren't that bothered about it and carried on playing our little game with them. Cos a cosh in the hand doesn't make up for a lack of brains in the head, or so we thought.

But then last week they caught Ferret. It was one evening. He was on his way to the Volksgarten to meet us. They were lying in wait for him right in the middle of Ehrenfeld. He didn't suspect a thing, cos they haven't dared show their faces there for months, so he walked right into their trap.

They really hate him cos he never can resist getting to a safe distance then yelling out some parting shot every time we've hoodwinked them. He's just got a big mouth and that's not always good, as he found out last week.

Five or six of them grabbed him and just started whacking him with their sticks without warning. He didn't even have the chance to defend himself. All he could do was keep his arms over his face. But they just kept on. Even when he was already on the ground. They kept on kicking him till they were exhausted. Then they swanned off and left him there.

We almost didn't recognize him the next day. His face was swollen and black and blue, he could hardly see and couldn't speak properly either. The girls were dead shocked. But Flint was boiling with anger. I think he feels kind of responsible for seeing that nothing happens to any of us. It was like they'd beaten him up. And in the middle of Ehrenfeld! That really rubbed him up the wrong way.

"They'll be sorry for this," he said. "Yes, they'll be damned sorry."

He and Knuckles planned our revenge. They scouted out the route the patrols take. Since they beat Ferret up, they've been marching through Ehrenfeld again nearly every evening and that really stinks. These are our streets, Flint says, our patch, and there's no way we can allow outsiders to feel at home here. Specially not those patrol idiots.

*Yesterday evening, we met at the Neptune Pool. We
kept the girls and Goethe out of it, and Ferret too, of course.
There were five of us: Flint, Knuckles, Lanky, Tom and me.*

*Flint had got hold of some knuckledusters and he
handed them out. It felt funny to hold mine at first. I'd
never used anything like that. I'd never been part of
anything like this before. Planned, like an ambush, I mean.
Fighting cos you have to defend yourself, or cos you blow
your top, sure, everyone does. But this was different. I was
this close to asking Flint if he was really sure about doing
this. But the others looked so determined I didn't want to
make a fool of myself. I think Tom felt the same. So we took
the knuckledusters and kept our traps shut.*

*Flint said the patrol always comes down Venloer, over
Neptunplatz, down Vogelsanger to Grünerweg, to the
station and back to town down Subbelrather. We lurked
behind the station, waiting for them. There's hardly anyone
about at that time and there are a few bushes to hide in.*

*We soon heard the clack of their boots, and then
there they were. They stopped right in front of us to light
cigarettes. It was just what we'd been waiting for and
we jumped them. They were taken completely by surprise.
Course they never dreamt anyone'd dare take them on
now they've got their truncheons. But they didn't even get
to draw them, Flint, Knuckles and Lanky were on them
so fast.*

*Tom and me, we jumped out after them, and the next
minute we were right in the thick of it. At first I was kind*

of scared to join in properly, but then one of the patrol whacked me over the head and that riled me up and I hit him back. And then the thing ran its course. We did what we could, Tom and me, but Flint and Knuckles did most of the work. Knuckles stood there solid as a rock, always on the same spot, dishing out one massive punch after another. And Flint ran round harrying them like a wolf—until none of them was left standing.

Then we beat it. Tom came off the worst of us, he was bleeding pretty badly. The rest of us just had a few knocks and Lanky had a black eye, but nothing serious. We ran arm in arm through the streets, singing our songs at the tops of our voices: "We march along the Rhine and Ruhr, fighting for our freedom. We'll smash the patrols and free the streets—Edelweiss, hooray!"

Lights went on everywhere. People threw open their windows and nagged at us not to make such a racket. But we didn't care, we just kept on singing. Boy, we were over the moon! Specially Flint.

"There, lads," he said, "we've avenged Ferret. And the patrol will think ten times now before setting foot in Ehrenfeld again."

I woke with a jump a few times in the night, reliving the scenes from the fight. I still remember the first time I hit out with that knuckleduster. The work at Ostermann has made me pretty strong over the last year and I heard the crunch as it connected with his jaw. The thought of it makes me shudder. But there you go. What they did to Ferret was *much worse. I think they got what they deserved. Yes. I reckon we had every right to do what we did.*

24th April 1942

We haven't seen hide nor hair of the patrols since we gave them that pasting. I wouldn't have thought it would be that easy but apparently we've taken the fight out of them.

"They won't be back," Flint said yesterday. "They've had enough. And if they do show their faces, the days of hiding from them are over, once and for all. Even if we meet them in the street in broad daylight, so what? What we did to them once, we can do again any time. There's no need to be scared any more, folks!"

I think he's right. Tom and me, we're fifteen now, some of the others have turned sixteen already. We work hard every day, so we're more than a match for the patrols. Why should we crap our pants at the sight of them? We've often sat around over the last few days, stocking up ideas of what to do to them if they show up on our patch again.

We don't mince our words about anything now. If anyone greets us on the street with "Heil Hitler!", we say, "No, heal him yourself!" And we've come up with nicknames for the bigwigs. We call Hitler "Toothbrush". Goebbels is "the Gerbil", and we call Göring "Christmas Tree" cos he's always dripping with decorations. We say

*it loud enough for everyone to hear. Cos it's fun to make
people angry. Some folks grin when they hear us, but lots
of them get hopping mad. It's interesting. You just have to
say one little word and the reaction instantly tells you who
you're dealing with.*

*Anyway, we're doing fine at the moment. We've got
what we wanted: the patrols have gone. No one's telling
us what to do or what not to do after work. We're our own
bosses. And why shouldn't it stay that way? The Nazis have
enough to do with their war and the Jews and whatever else
they're planning. They haven't got time for people like us.
Have they?*

26th May 1942

*Yesterday and the day before, it was our Whitsun trip to
the Felsensee again. It was meant to be the high point of the
year, like last time. And it was at first. But then it turned
into a total catastrophe.*

*On Sunday morning, we met up and set off. Took the
train to Oberkassel and then walked into the Siebengebirge.
The weather was the best. As we climbed, we sang the
Felsensee song: "Lying lonely and alone within their walls
of stone are the quiet, peaceful waters of our lakeside
home from home. At the Felsensee, we pirates of the noble
Edelweiss meet with our pretty lasses from Cologne upon
the Rhine." Then there was the lake below us, and as we*

headed down the path, we struck up our new battle cry that we'd come up with after the victory over the patrol: "We're champions of the world, the EP from Ehrenfeld"—EP stands for Edelweiss Pirates, obviously. Course there was a big fuss as we marched down to the others, cos they didn't know the chant yet.

I suddenly realized how much had changed since the first time we went to the lake. Then we were new boys, Tom and me. We were shy and scared and everyone could smell ten miles off that we were fresh out of the HJ.

This time was different. These days, we wear our pirate get-up like it's the most natural thing in the world. We've got long hair and walk tall. And we know lots of the others now from our weekend trips. No one would dream of making fun of us. They greeted us like we'd always been part of their group. As if we'd grown up over the year.

We spent the day swimming, eating, scrapping and getting up to all kinds of larking about, whatever came into our heads. When it got dark, we sat around the campfire talking about what had happened recently. There were a couple of lads from Wuppertal there, a year or two older than us. They reckoned that round their way, the SS are dealing with people like us in person now.

Course that made us prick up our ears. "The SS!" Flint said. "What have you lot been up to?"

"What d'you mean, 'been up to'? We've done nothing, man! Just the usual. But the patrols can't manage us any more. So now they're sending the SS."

"So what does that mean?" Floss asked.

"What do you think it means? It means trouble. There's nothing they won't do, and they don't give a damn how old you are. They just beat the hell out of you. Compared to a tangle with them, a battle with the patrols is a walk in the park. Just make sure you never cross paths with them!"

"We had a fight with a patrol recently," Lanky said. "Haven't shown their faces since."

Another of the Wuppertalers shook his head. "Not a good sign," he said. "Don't go thinking they'll leave you be. If the patrols aren't coming round any more, something worse is on its way."

That didn't sound good at all. They told us about their experiences with the SS and that really made us feel queasy.

"And another thing," one of the Wuppertalers said. "Don't think anyone'll help if it gets serious. People are chicken. They're afraid of the Gestapo and the special courts and all that. They just creep around the place, terrified of saying or doing the wrong thing."

"Right," said Flint. "That's why people haven't got much time for us either."

The others didn't know what he meant. So he explained. "Most of 'em aren't bad people, right? Deep down, they're probably against the stuff that's happening too. But they daren't do a thing about it. So they feel guilty. And every time they see people like us, it makes 'em realize what cowards they are. So they'd rather not have to see us. I tell you, they wouldn't give a damn if we just vanished."

He nudged Knuckles, who was sitting next to him. "What d'you reckon?"

"They 'ate us cos we're free," rumbled Knuckles.

"Exactly! That's it. Knuckles has spoken."

The others laughed. What Flint had said sounded plausible. Only one person—I think he was from Dortmund—had any objections.

"But for us it's easy to be free," he said. "We've got nothing to lose."

"How d'you mean?" Flint asked.

"Well, think about it. They need us as cheap slave labour so they won't take our jobs away. They can't take anything else off us either—obviously, cos we don't own a thing. And we don't have any wives or kids they can hold over us. But imagine being a bloke with a house an' a family an' a super job. He could lose everything if he blabbed. So he shuts his trap and ducks away."

A few people objected at first, but in the end, everyone had to admit he was right.

"Could be," one of the Wuppertalers said. "But luckily I don't have the same problems as a big shot like that. And I don't care about them either."

We could agree on that. We didn't feel like talking any more, so Goethe got out his guitar and began to play. Every time I listen to him, I get swept away. All he's got are those six little strings on that thing, but it's like magic—the notes sound like they come from a different world. It's funny: the others, who don't know him so well, like to take the mick a bit. Cos he doesn't talk like us and he's got such soft hands. But whenever he starts playing, that all stops. Then he's king. Then nobody laughs. And it was the same that evening. We just squatted there, staring into the fire, and forgot everything around us.

That night we slept under the stars like last year. We had lookouts posted around the lake cos we thought the HJ might show up again but it was all quiet. So we had a field day bad-mouthing them. We thought they must be too scared cos they were still feeling the hiding from last year in their bones.

But of course we'd gloated too soon. The moment we got on the train back to Cologne yesterday afternoon, we noticed a couple of funny-looking types on the station, hanging around the place, watching us. We didn't think anything of it at first, but when we got into Cologne, we realized why they'd been standing there.

The train pulled into the station and stopped but the doors didn't open. Nobody was allowed off. After a few minutes, a huge troop of SS men marched across the platform. When we saw them, we feared the worst. For the whole journey, we'd been making a huge racket and singing our songs, but suddenly it was dead quiet.

The SS men got on at the front and the back and combed the train. Not just for us, of course. There were other Edelweiss Pirates from other parts of town. Must've been about fifty. All coming back from the Felsensee—or wherever they'd been.

Our clothes made us easy to spot. The SS flushed out one group after another and ran them off the train. They had sub-machine guns so nobody dared do anything about it. A couple of the people on the train clapped. Said they were welcome to make short work of a rabble like us. I guess our songs annoyed them. Or they didn't like our hair or the way we look. Or they were just Nazis.

They herded us together on the platform. Some of the SS had their guns at the ready and were pointing them at us. My knees were knocking. It's a damn funny feeling looking down a barrel like that.

Then we had to leave the station. Anyone who walked too slowly got a whack in the back that you wouldn't forget in a hurry. Outside, we had to get into vans and they took us to the closest police station.

They were expecting us. We had to stand in a long corridor, lined up against the wall, no one was allowed to sit down or say anything. The SS men stood opposite us, watching, then we were called into one of the rooms. Always alone, one at a time. It was pretty fierce standing there, waiting, cos the whole time we could hear shouts and screams, there were often slaps or a dull blow. Lots of us came out with bleeding faces.

It seemed to last a lifetime. Eventually it was my turn and I went in. Inside there was a policeman sitting behind his desk and I had to stand in front of him. Still wasn't allowed to sit down. There were two SS men in the room too, who came to stand right behind me.

The policeman wanted to know my name and where I live. I didn't want to tell him cos we'd sworn not to give it away. So first I asked him what I was accused of.

But that was a mistake. I'd barely finished speaking when one of the SS grabbed me and twisted my head to one side and the other boxed my ears so I saw stars. Screamed at me to shut my mouth and only answer what I was asked.

The policeman waited till I could more or less see again and then repeated his question. What choice did I have? I didn't fancy the blokes breaking all my bones. So I told them my name, where I live and where I work.

Then he wanted to know my HJ unit. I said I wasn't in the HJ. I could feel the bully behind me winding up, but the cop stopped him. I don't think it was cos he felt sorry for me. Probably just wanted to knock off early.

"Don't you know you need permission from the HJ to travel?" he asked.

"No," I said, "that's news to me. But now I know, I'll remember that."

Then he wanted to know all kinds of things about me and the others: where we meet, what we call ourselves, if we're in touch with other groups and so on.

"No idea," I said. "I don't really know the others. I just heard about the meeting and went along cos I was nosy. But now I know it's not allowed, I certainly won't do it again."

I acted gormless and luckily he at least half believed me. Then he sentenced me to juvenile detention. So I wouldn't get up to any more silly pranks in future, he said. Properly, only the courts are allowed to do that, but they're not so strict at the moment cos of the war. "Expedited proceedings for juvenile detention" they call it.

So we had to stay there. Apart from the girls, who they sent home. Not alone of course, there was a policeman with them. He was supposed to lecture their parents on taking better care of their daughters in future and making extra certain they weren't hanging around with scum like us.

We were split between several police stations cos there weren't enough cells in that one. Had to sit there all night and all day today. The cells are tiny and there's just a plank bed with a blanket, and nothing else. The only thing to eat was dry bread. And to stop you getting bored, a cop comes in now and then and slaps you about a bit.

But that wasn't such a big deal. The worst thing was that they sent us off with a haircut. Crew cut! And they let us go on condition that we report to the HJ immediately or there'd be even more trouble.

When we finally got out, we felt pretty drained. We were furious at the way they'd treated us. Like we were total filth. Snapping at us and hitting out when we had no chance to defend ourselves! All we were left with was a kind of cold rage that we didn't even know what to do with.

We talked about where we should go from here. The more we thought about it, the more subdued we got. Cos the very thing we've always wanted to avoid has happened.

They know who we are and where to find us. From now on, we'll have no peace from them.

But we promised ourselves one thing: none of us will go back to the HJ. They'd have to bring tanks and drag us off there by force. But they won't. After all, they need the tanks at the front.

And that's a long way away.

A week later, I visited old Mr Gerlach again. By then, I'd read the first pages of his diary and, as I sat at his table, I could feel how nervously he was waiting for my opinion. He was trying to hide it by bustling about—at least as much as he could at his age. But he avoided asking me directly. He was too considerate for that, as I'd come to realize.

"I was wondering, how many people have actually read the diary?" I asked when he finally sat down again.

He looked at me in astonishment. "Nobody," he said.

"You mean—I'm the first? But why?"

He raised his hands then let them sink down again. "After the war, nobody wanted to hear that stuff. Everyone was occupied with looking forward and building a new life for themselves. Nobody wanted to be reminded of that time. So eventually I shut the book away. And, over time, I forgot about it myself."

"I can't believe that."

"But that's how it was, whether you believe it or not. I had my hands full just getting by. The past just got in the way. Besides, it hurt too much to think about it. All the friends I'd lost and would never find again! I didn't want that. I didn't touch the book for decades."

"But you didn't throw it away either."

He smiled. "No, I didn't have the heart to do that. And now I'm glad of it. After I stopped working, the memories came back, one after another, and now I think about them day and night." He stared at the plate of biscuits he'd put on the table, and then suddenly laughed. "You know, it's funny. These days I can't always remember what I ate for lunch yesterday or did in the evening. But events from back then—over sixty years ago—I can remember every detail of them again now. Isn't that odd?"

I didn't really know what he was talking about. I let my eyes roam around his room and I noticed a few things I hadn't spotted on my first visit. Mainly that there were no pictures of him. Not a single one.

How strange that is, I thought. I know him the way he is today. And, through his diary, I know him from when he was young. But I don't know a thing about all the decades in between. It's like a long journey, when you only notice the departure and the arrival.

"Didn't you ever get married?" I asked. "Or have children?"

A moment later, I could have bitten my tongue out. He looked at me and his eyes were suddenly so sad that I wished I'd never asked such a stupid question.

"I'm sorry," I said. "It's none of my business."

He shook his head and shrugged it off. "No, no, don't worry. I never married. Wasn't an option any more. And I've got no children either. Although..." The grief vanished out of his eyes, "I did have a child once, all the same. In a way, at least. But that was a long time ago."

He crossed his arms and looked out of the window. For a while he sat there like that without moving. It was only when I pulled the diary out of my rucksack and laid it on the table that he seemed alert again.

"Have you finished it already?" he asked.

"No," I said, and opened it at the page I'd got to. When he saw, he looked disappointed.

"That's not very far. Do you find it boring?"

"No! It's not boring!"

"What then?"

"You mean, why am I reading so slowly?" I picked the book up and packed it away again. "There's another reason. I'll tell you when I've finished it, OK?"

He sighed, then suddenly had a coughing fit. It shook his whole body. I sat there, not knowing what to do. Eventually, it passed. He looked at me and nodded.

"Don't be too long about it," he said. "Do you hear me?"

31st May 1942

So now it's here: the war. Arrived last night. Right in the middle of our city.

It was all so unreal. Cos it was actually the most beautiful spring night you could imagine. Mild, with the smell of blossom in the air. We were in the Volksgarten, in the bit we call the rose garden. There are flowers there in all colours, and lots of hidden corners among the bushes where nobody can find us.

We sat there till late at night, chatting. Since the business with the SS we've been at home as little as possible, especially at the weekend. Like we agreed, none of us has gone to the HJ, and we don't want them to come and nick us for that. Now they've got our names and addresses.

That was the main thing we talked about yesterday evening: how to make sure they don't get us. But Flint had another thing on his mind: how we can get our revenge for the way we were treated at the police station. What happened there really rubbed him up the wrong way, even more than the rest of us. He hates it like poison if he can't pay someone back for doing a thing like that to him.

We were still in the middle of it when suddenly the sirens went off. It was after midnight, I think. We didn't take much notice at first cos they've been wailing every

*couple of nights for the last few months. Usually a false
alarm. Or a couple of British bombers come and attack
some factory on the edge of town. Nothing much has ever
happened here in Ehrenfeld.*

*But last night was different, as we soon realized. The
thunder and rattle of the flak started up almost at the
same moment as the sirens. Not just in a few places like
usual but everywhere. There were hundreds of searchlights
in the sky, the flak was like a barrier round the city. There
was a crash that went right through you. We ran out of
the bush we were sitting under, onto the big lawn in the
middle of the Volksgarten. We barely beat the bombers.
You could hear their deep roar—it was a thousand times
louder than we'd heard in earlier raids. When you looked
up, they were just everywhere. The whole sky was full
of them.*

*Then the bombs dropped and there was a hell of a noise.
It seemed never-ending, all across the whole city. The air
trembled and the ground shook, even in the Volksgarten,
where we were standing. At first we were scared and
wondered whether to hide. But then we noticed that there
wasn't anything coming down around us, so we stayed
where we were. It was a terrible sight. Before long, there
were fires everywhere, the whole sky was red with flames. A
real sea of fire. Everywhere we turned.*

*I don't know how long the raid lasted. Then the noise
faded, the bombers flew away, the flak stopped. Suddenly it
was quiet, all you could hear was the crackle of the flames.*

Ehrenfeld was all red too. We thought of our mums and ran.

None of us will ever forget what we saw last night. It was hell. There were flames shooting out of houses everywhere. Roofs fell in, glowing rubble was falling like rain onto the road. The glass sprayed out of some windows, burning beams blocked the way. It was so hot you could hardly breathe.

Somehow we managed to get through to Ehrenfeld. Whole streets were on fire. Once we saw people who hadn't got out in time, jumping from an upstairs floor. They were on fire like living torches. I can't think about how many must've been buried under the rubble.

We split up—everyone wanted to get home as quick as we could. Tom and me ran to Klarastrasse. There were a few buildings on fire there too, but luckily not all of them. People were out in the street trying to put out the fires. Standing in a long line, passing buckets of water along. Mum and Tom's mum were there too. We were so glad to see them. Went over and joined them in the chain. It didn't help much: so little water against so many flames. But nobody was thinking about that. Everyone just wanted to do something—however pointless.

We slaved away till morning when we couldn't go on. By then there were only a few small fires among the rubble. They weren't worth the effort, they'd go out by themselves.

People went home, just not Tom and me. We met the others and walked around the streets with them. The sun never came out properly. There were such thick black clouds of smoke in the sky it didn't stand a chance. Wherever we went there was a kind of biting, sweetish smell of fire. It makes you sick if you get too much of it.

We saw bad things. Lorries, full to the top with burnt and charred people. They were unrecognizable. It shook us when they drove past. And we thought: now the war's come for us too. Lots of the older people here in Ehrenfeld warned that what the bigwigs had done would come back to bite us. We didn't want to believe them at first. Now we know they were right. And, who knows, people were saying today: maybe this is just the start.

18th June 1942

Since the bombing night, people here in Ehrenfeld are furious. And not even with the British who did it. After all, we started the raids, they say. And so you can't complain if it comes back at you.

No, they're furious cos things are lousy and nobody's helping them. So many people have lost their flats or had family killed in the raid. And what's being done for them? Nothing! Some stupid van came round the streets the day after with hot soup for everyone. That's it. Might as well not have bothered, or so lots of people are saying.

On the radio they announced that the Brits suffered such severe losses during the raid that they'll never be back.

But the people who listen to foreign stations are secretly saying something else. There were over a thousand planes, so we're now calling it the "thousand-bomber raid". And our flak hardly caught any of them. They'll be back, sure as eggs is eggs.

Some people remember what Göring said. Back when the war started: you could call him Meier if a single British bomber turned up here. So that's what everyone's calling him—and it's certainly not kindly meant.

And the raid also showed that there aren't enough bunkers for everyone in Ehrenfeld. They don't care, people say, only scum live here. And they whisper that the real bigwigs—Grohé and co.—get real luxury bunkers. Where they party and live the high life while everything around them is burning to ashes and us poor sods don't know where to go to stay safe.

Anyway, those are the things making people angry. You can really feel it when you walk down the road. But it's not an open anger, more something helpless. Nobody will shout about what they really think—that just doesn't happen. People only whisper it at home or with people they've known all their life.

Cos it's not just the anger getting worse. It's the fear too. Somehow it feels like there are more spies. People round here have always been suspicious of newcomers. But there've been cases where local people have grassed someone up to the Gestapo cos they had a score to settle. Since then, nobody trusts anyone.

So the fear's bigger than the anger, I think. But for how long? Will that ever change?

Almost every night's a bombing night now. The same every time: first the sirens howl, then the flak thunders, then the bombs drop. People jump out of bed, run into the street and try to find shelter in some bunker or cellar. They cower down there, hoping that a direct hit won't bury them—and that their building will be left standing of course. It's pretty hard, especially for the elderly who can't move quickly any more.

The bunkers are important meeting places for us Edelweiss Pirates. Specially the one on Takuplatz here in Ehrenfeld, which is kind of our new regular spot. We're there almost every evening and often stay all night long. We meet lots of people from the other groups and swap news with them. It's almost our home from home now.

But we never go inside the bunker, not even when the biggest bombs are dropping. We always stay out, somewhere in front of it. Because of the air raid wardens. They're in charge of the bunkers and keep everything in order. And they keep their ears open. Cos it's been known for someone down there to lose their nerve and say what they really think. Even if it's just something like "Won't this damn war ever end?" That's enough. A few days later, an invitation to the Gestapo drops through their letter box. For "subversion of the war effort".

Course it's dangerous being outside when the bombs drop. But we say to ourselves: our lives are dangerous anyway. Any moment could be the last, and you might cop it anywhere. So what the heck? Why not at least make the most of the time we've got left? There's fresh air up there, we can breathe freely, nobody's checking on us, while downstairs it's stuffy and dusty and infested with spies.

And anyway, if one of the big, high-explosive bombs smashes through down there, no bunker'll help either way. Then everything falls in and you're buried. And the idea of being buried alive down there is about the worst thing we can imagine. So we'd rather stay outside. Better cop it up there and die out in the open than snuff it down in the dirt like rats.

And I've realized something else lately: in a way, the raids aren't even so bad for us, funny as that sounds. Cos since they started, the SS and HJ have got their hands full bringing order to the chaos and keeping people in line. So at the moment we're not so important to them. Normally, they'd be after us like the devil—now they know who we are and seeing that we didn't go back to the HJ like they ordered. But this has bought us some time.

It's funny. We're probably the only ones who benefit from the bombs at all.

I've been at Ostermann over a year now. In that time, it's got worse and worse at work, specially for us apprentices. We start in the morning and stay till late in the evening. For as long as it suits the gaffer. Sixty hours a week is normal, but sometimes it's even more.

And the targets we have to hit keep getting stricter. We're making stuff for the army and the navy. So it's always more, faster, better. Which means there are often accidents. People are tired and not paying attention. A few fingers have been lost in the last few months. Fortunately none of mine.

Us apprentices don't see why we should jump through hoops so that the blokes at the front can blast each other away better. Like Flint and Knuckles said. So we slack off a bit when no one's looking. Or take a day off when it gets too much—easy to make up an illness. Or one of the machines might stop working cos a tool happened to fall into a bit that no one can get at. We're not short of ideas. Specially on the days when we've had a few too many boxed ears. Then we're really at our best.

There's no point getting the older blokes involved. They're wired differently from us. For them, it's dead important to do good work. They'd almost kill themselves trying to meet the piecework. Otherwise, we get on well, but there's no joking with them on this one. It's just a different generation, I reckon.

Yesterday, the big boss got us all together in the main hall and gave us a lecture. We were behind on our targets, he said, and he wasn't putting up with that any more. After all, the reputation of the company was on the line. In some groups—and he gave us apprentices a particular look when he said that—efficiency was so bad that it couldn't be an accident. So watch out: if we were deliberately holding up production, that'd be sabotage, and there's the death penalty for that. Anyone caught in the act would be reported—and whatever happened after that would be our own fault. There was an extra snappy "Heil Hitler!" and then he let us go.

We trotted back to work.

"Just cut the nonsense out," one of the older ones whispered, with a threatening glare at us apprentices. "Sabotage is a bloody serious thing and if you get busted, it won't just be you who're for it, but the rest of us too. Anyway, it's pointless. You're just putting us in danger!"

Today I kept on thinking about that and then I got angry. Why was he talking about danger? We could do loads more and nobody would be in any danger. We just need to be united—and stick together. That's what's missing.

16th September 1942

Recently, we've spent almost every night at the bunker. The girls too. It's warm enough—and there's nothing to

*keep us at home. Our mums are pretty decent but we can't
really talk to them. Not about important stuff anyway.
They just don't understand what we're doing. They'd
rather we stayed with them instead of hanging around,
getting into trouble. But they can't tell us what to do these
days. We earn our own money. So we can do what we
want.*

*There's often a funny mood round the bunker in the
evenings. Around nine or ten, a heap of oldies turn up, all
from Ehrenfeld. Most of them have suitcases and deckchairs
and set themselves up outside the entrance on spec. If there's
a real alarm, they're the first in and get the best spots. We
always sit a little to one side and laugh at them. But it's
just for fun, actually we don't mind them.*

*Yesterday evening, when it was dark, the sirens went
off again. The oldies headed into the bunker and then the
others came running. Most of them sleep in their clothes
now and have suitcases by their beds so they can get out
quicker. We stayed outside, as usual, and then there wasn't
much up. They lobbed a bit at Kalk and Mühlheim across
the Rhine but it was quiet round our way. Soon over, and
after an hour or so, the bunker was empty again.*

*"Reckon that's it for tonight," Flint said. "They've
never come more than once a night."*

*"Such gentlemen, the British," Ferret said. "Like I've
always said, they still know how to behave."*

*"So explain this to me," Tilly said. "If they're such
gentlemen, why do they only bomb the poor areas and not*

*where the rich folks live? That's a pretty dirty trick, don't
you think?"*

*She was right. Here in Ehrenfeld and Nippes, whole
streets are bombed to rubble while some of the posher areas
have barely been hit. Can't be coincidence.*

*Lanky reckoned it's to do with the war industries. They
want to hit the factories—and the workers. Cos if there are
no workers, they can't produce anything. And if nothing
gets produced, the army'll be done for, any day now.*

*"I think there's something else behind it too," said Floss.
"These leaflets that the Tommies keep dropping after their
attacks: have you ever read one?"*

*Before we could answer, she reached under her blouse
and there she had one. When Tilly saw it she almost fainted.*

*"Man, Floss, throw that away! If they find it, you're
finished!"*

*"But they won't find it," Floss said. "I'm keeping it
somewhere no respectable SS man will look. And definitely
no scrubby lout from the HJ."*

*Then she read what was on the leaflet: "England's
offer: justice for all, even the Germans; punishment for the
guilty; economic equality and security. England's demand:
the German people must themselves take action to free
themselves from Hitler's gangster rule. The German people
have the choice."*

*Tom, who was sitting next to her, gave her a sideways
look. "You mean they're hoping for some kind of people's
uprising?"*

"Yes! That'd make their lives easier and they could save the bother of the war. And I'm telling you, that's why they're bombing working areas. Cos they think they'll have the best chance of success here. And that's true, people are getting angrier with the Nazis with every raid."

She slipped the leaflet away again. We sat there awhile with the idea running through our heads. Everyone thought what she said made sense.

"What happens to the leaflets anyway?" Goethe asked at some point.

"They send the HJ round," Flint answered. "Saw 'em once. They gather the things and tear 'em up."

Lanky looked thoughtfully at him. "So—what if we got there first? Snap the things up and shove them in people's letter boxes. Everywhere, in every block?"

"Got any other bright ideas?" Ferret tapped his forehead. "Might as well ring the Gestapo's doorbell and ask to be let in. They'll wipe the floor with us!"

"Why?" Flint said. "They'd have to find out who did it first, and they won't. We'll do it by night and post lookouts. I don't think it's a bad idea."

Knuckles thought the same. But the rest of us weren't convinced. Tilly reckoned that just when we'd managed to get some peace from them, we shouldn't go stirring up more trouble. Tom, Goethe and Maja wanted to keep on the safe side and, in the end, it was too much even for Floss.

"I think we should only do something like that if everyone agrees," she said to Flint and Lanky. "Cos we *belong together, don't we? And either everyone should be in on a thing like this—or no one."*

And she was damn well right. Even Flint had to agree to that, and so we didn't talk about it any more. We were awake for another hour or two, then we settled down to sleep.

The others dropped off pretty quickly, but I couldn't get to sleep for ages, thinking about all kinds of stuff. Tom was snoring on one side of me, and I could hear Tilly breathing on the other side. I kept thinking about everything that's happened recently. So much has changed. Everything's more serious and stricter. Not so funny and easy-going as last year.

I sat up and watched the others. They were all in a heap. Tangled on top of each other or next to each other, wherever they'd fallen asleep. It made me laugh. Now we really are a bit like pirates, I thought. Homeless. Tossed to and fro like a small boat on the high seas. But it's OK. At least we've got each other. We're friends and we stick together. And that's more than most people can say.

Especially in shit times like these.

By then it was the middle of December. While everyone else was getting into a Christmassy mood, I'd got into the habit of popping in on old Mr Gerlach every couple of days. The home where he lived seemed as inhospitable as ever to me, but I no longer paid any attention to the smell or the grumpy porter or the intrusive house rules or the other things that had alarmed me on my first visit. I began to feel that there was something linking the old man and me—however different we were. Some kind of connection that I couldn't explain.

His diary entries fascinated me. I tried to imagine what he must have looked like back then—as a boy. But when I asked him if he had a photo from that time, he shook his head.

"We didn't take photos," was all he said. "We had to promise Flint that. And we kept our word."

I wondered what it must feel like to look back on such a long life. Was the boy you'd been sixty years ago a stranger to you now—almost like another person? Or was there something, deep inside you, in some small, secret place, that never changed, that always remained the same from birth to death, like your name or the colour of your eyes or the birthmark on your back? Were you still familiar with yourself after all that time? Could you still recognize yourself? And who was the old man more similar to: some other oldie from today or the boy from back then? All these thoughts went through my head whenever I read the young Josef Gerlach's diary and then met him the next day as an old man.

I remember one of those days particularly well. I was sitting on my own in the room for some time while old Mr Gerlach disappeared into the bathroom. I thought about how laborious and time-consuming even the simplest things became when you were old. Every walk to the toilet was like a mini quest, kind of the adventure of the day. At first, I'd been revolted by these side effects of ageing, just like the smell in the entrance hall. But by then I was used to it, it didn't bother me any more.

As I was sitting at the table, waiting for the old man to come back, I looked out of the window, down into the garden of the residential home. There was snow lying on the lawn and the trees, only the paths had been cleared. It was rare for anyone to be out for a stroll there, but that day I saw a figure among the bushes. I saw somebody standing there, looking up at me and, although I couldn't make out their face, which was hidden by a coat and scarf, I got the feeling that they were looking me in the eye.

I turned away and flicked through a newspaper that was lying on the table. After a while, I looked out into the garden again. The figure was still there. I stood up and walked over to the balcony door, opened it and looked out.

But when I leant over the railings, they'd gone. I scanned the whole garden but couldn't see them anywhere. Not a soul in sight.

I shook my head in surprise. Had I started seeing things? I looked down once more and then headed back into the flat. Old Mr Gerlach was waiting for me.

4th February 1943

At the moment, people can only talk about one thing:
Stalingrad. Our soldiers have been bottled up in there.
Now they've had to surrender and become POWs. Them
that are left, that is. Most are dead. Shot, starved, frozen.
Horrible deaths. Nobody can imagine what they went
through. Nobody wants to imagine it.

There are rumours that most of them died for nothing.
They say the Russians invited them to surrender ages ago.
The generals wanted to cos it was all hopeless—only Hitler
didn't. "A German soldier never surrenders," he said, and
he sent them all to their deaths instead. People are furious
when they hear those things.

On the radio they're talking about "heroes' deaths"
again and that now we'll show the Russians. But nobody
wants to hear that. I don't know what it's like in other
places, but here in Ehrenfeld, the people have stopped
believing that stuff. We knew it from the start, they say.
That you can't beat the Russians. Now we're getting our
comeuppance.

Nobody dreams of the final victory any more—those
times are over. They say that all the top brass are doing is
putting off the rude awakening. And that from now on,
every defeat is like a victory. Cos then it'll be over sooner.

24th February 1943

*There's bad news. Some students in Munich were executed
for secretly giving out leaflets against the Nazis and the
war. The "White Rose" they were called. A caretaker
grassed them up, then the Gestapo collared them. The
People's Court sentenced them to death for undermining
morale and high treason.*

*"Now we know what Goebbels meant," said Tom when
we met at the bunker today. "About shirkers. And people
losing their heads."*

*We'd heard the speech he was talking about on the
radio. Last week. There was no shortage of advertising
for it. Apparently, the Nazis have noticed that morale is
a bit low. After Stalingrad and the constant air raids.
Goebbels tried to play everything down. What the British
say in their leaflets is nonsense, he said. And then he asked
the public if they believe in victory and if they want total
war and have faith in the Führer and the whole works.
Every time, they roared, "Yes!" In the end, he asked if
they agree that any shirkers and anyone who has anything
against the war should lose their heads. And again they
screamed, "Yes!"*

*"Watch out, before long, they'll stop at nothing," Flint
said. "Anyone who protests will be for the chop. From now
on they'll be lining them up."*

*"Did you hear that that lot in Munich didn't just give
out leaflets, they also painted slogans on house walls?" asked*

116

Floss. "'Down with Hitler!' and other stuff too. Crept out at night and wrote it in secret."

"Bloody brave of them," Flint said. "Even though they were students. Wouldn't have thought it of 'em."

We're not that fond of students. Cos they'd got into the grammar schools. And cos we could never have got to university like them, no matter how hard we tried. But what those students in Munich did was amazing. It was pretty good work, we're all agreed on that.

"D'you know why they called themselves the White Rose?" Tilly asked.

"I think it's because they used to be in the old German Youth Movement, which had a white flower as its symbol," Goethe answered. "They probably got it from there. Just like our Edelweiss."

Tilly's eyes were wide. "You mean, we're kind of related to them?"

"Yes," Goethe said, "kind of."

15th March 1943

What we did caused a massive stink. More than we thought. On one hand that's good, cos shaking people up was the point of it all. But on the other hand: who knows what might happen now!

It all started last week. We were sitting outside the bunker and talking about what we want to do this year.

Then the sirens blared and people ran in from all over the place, as usual. But it was a false alarm. After just a couple of minutes, there was the all-clear and everyone could go again. Some of them were swearing like troopers. You could really see it bubbling up inside them.

"Hey guys, take cover!" Ferret said. "That old boy back there's about to blow. He's as overheated as a fire bomb!"

He pointed at a man coming out of the bunker with his suitcase, grumbling away loudly to himself. His wife was walking beside him with two camp chairs, and hissed at him to be quiet. But he said he was in no mood to be quiet, damn it, and carried on. The others trotted past him. Nobody dared look at him.

"Typical," said Flint, pointing at them. "Don't see anything, don't hear anything, don't know anything. But have you noticed? The mood today is crappier than ever. And it gets a notch crappier with every alarm."

We watched the people as they left. They really were in a mighty bad mood. But at the same time, most of them looked like they didn't care any more. Like they'd already resigned themselves to their fate.

"P'raps it's time to lend a hand," Lanky said. "With morale."

"What d'you mean?" Floss asked.

"Well, you heard Goebbels, didn't you? With his talk of total war. It's not hard to imagine what that means: they'll carry on. To the bitter end. Till there's not a wall left standing. Till everyone's had it up to here. And I don't

118

think we should just look on. Or shall we sit around here and wait to cop it too? I'm telling you, if this isn't the time to do something about it, then it never will be!"

That hit home—it was quiet for a bit after that. We squatted there, thinking about what he'd said. Somehow, everyone felt he was right. But we didn't exactly want to admit it. Or that's how I felt, anyway.

"Oh, I dunno," Tilly said in the end. "Remember what happened to that lot in Munich. There's always some swine who'll snitch on you. And then we'd be for it! If they caught us, they'd kill us. They don't care how old you are."

"Yes!" Goethe said, looking first at Lanky, then at Flint. "It doesn't bother them. Tilly's right. It's far too dangerous."

"Oh, dangerous!" Flint gestured scornfully. "Everything's dangerous, Goethe! Every day, and specially the nights. Nobody knows if we'll still be here tomorrow or lying under some heap of rubble. Or what the SS have in store for us if we carry on like we are now. So we might as well do something meaningful. I think Lanky's right."

"But what can we do?" Maja asked. We were surprised because normally she only listens, but that evening she joined in. "We don't know anyone. And people won't take us seriously. Or do you think they'll be interested in what kids like us have to say?"

"They won't know it's us," Lanky said. "We're not going to stand on a street corner with a megaphone. They'll find a couple of leaflets in their letter box. Or there'll be something painted on a wall in some underpass, in the morning when they go to work. They'll think it's somebody else entirely."

"All the same: a few slogans won't change anything," Ferret said. "What d'you think people'll do when they read them? D'you think they'll dig out their guns from the cupboard and start a revolution? Forget it! They're too chicken."

"Maybe," Lanky said. "But maybe not. Cos if the leaflets and slogans keep turning up, they'll see that there are people that the Nazis can't get at. Maybe it'll give them courage. Maybe it'll be like a little snowball that ends up as a whole avalanche."

Ferret wasn't convinced. But Floss looked kind of thoughtful as she listened to Lanky.

"You could be right," she said. "And besides, maybe it doesn't even matter if it changes anything. Maybe all that matters is doing something. For our own sakes, you see? Just for us."

We spent hours talking that evening, till late at night. In the end, what Floss had said settled it. Cos it's true: nobody knows what'll come of us or the stuff we do. We can't plan anything anyway, while there are bombs dropping round our ears practically every night. So the best thing is to do what we think's right. Whether it has any point or not. At any rate, then we'll be able to look ourselves in the eye. And there aren't many people nowadays who can say that.

In the end, we all saw it the same way, even Maja and Goethe and Ferret. We discussed what we actually wanted to do, and eventually settled on the thing Lanky had already suggested last year: collecting up the leaflets the Tommies drop and secretly delivering them. It's the simplest way, cos we don't know how to make leaflets ourselves. And we can't write such fancy texts. So we thought, why reinvent the wheel when it's already there?

The next raid was a couple of nights later. We waited till it was over and the people had vanished out of the bunker again. Then we made tracks. The leaflets usually come when everyone's busy putting out the fires. And that's what happened this time too. We ran this way and that across Ehrenfeld and gathered up any we could get our hands on. We didn't attract much attention. On bombing nights, people don't have any time to spare for the likes of us.

So last night was the night. We waited till after midnight cos there's usually nobody out and about then. Flint and Knuckles had taken all the leaflets and hidden them. They didn't tell us where, so that nobody could give it away if things got serious. Then they brought them back again and they were the two who slipped them in the letter boxes too. The rest of us stood guard. Up and down whatever street we were on and looking down all the side streets so no one would take us by surprise. Luckily all stayed quiet. We managed to cover the whole area either side of Venloer without any incident. Then Flint and Knuckles were out of leaflets so we scarpered.

When I got home from work today, all hell had broken loose. Our block warden had found one of the leaflets in his letter box. At first he thought they'd only been delivered to our building, so they must have been delivered by someone living there. But then he found out they'd turned up all over Ehrenfeld. I heard him questioning everyone in the building on whether they'd seen anything in the night. But nobody had. A few made it clear that they wouldn't tell him if they had. In the end, he left, red-faced, with the leaflets under his arm. "There'll be consequences for this!" he screamed.

Up in our flat, one of those leaflets was on the kitchen table. Mum must have brought it up from the letter box. I couldn't help grinning when I saw it. She asked me if I knew anything about the business. I said, "No, why?" But she's always spotted it if I lie to her, got some kind of sixth sense for it. She wanted to know if I had anything to do with it. When I said, "No, for God's sake, I'm not stupid," she had to sit down. She looked at me and I realized she was scared.

I said she shouldn't worry, nothing would happen to me. But that wasn't the way to calm her down. She sat there looking small and shrunk. Then she said I was sixteen now and old enough to know what I was doing. But I should promise to be careful for God's sake.

Ha, be careful! I thought. That's not exactly our strong point. But in the end I promised, so as to stop her worrying. When I left, I saw her slip the leaflet into a drawer. Right at the back, so nobody will see. But that was OK. She could have ripped it up.

17th April 1943

Horst's been back in Cologne for the last couple of days. His six years in Sonthofen are over. He's finished at the school, was one of the best in his year. Now he's going into the SS. That'll open every door to him, he says—just like he always wanted.

It was a strange feeling when I met him at the station. After all, we hadn't seen each other for nearly two years. He had his SS uniform on and at first I wanted to scram, like I always do when I see one of them. But then I realized that it was Horst inside it. He's eighteen now, but looks older. At first glance, I didn't even recognize my brother. But on a second look, yeah, he's still the same.

In the meantime I'd written to him that I'd quit the HJ and was hanging around with other people now. What kind of people and what we got up to I obviously kept to myself—not the stuff for a letter. He didn't answer. Which doesn't mean he doesn't care. No, I know him: he'd rather clear something like that up in person. Just the two of us. So I guessed what was coming.

Today he came to the flat with a couple of ration cards he'd got hold of. He's got good connections now, hasn't he? He pressed them into Mum's hand and sent her off

shopping. Told her to take her time and not hurry back—
he'd got something to discuss with me.

When we were alone, he tackled me. Wanted to know
what was wrong with me.

"Why?" I said. "What d'you mean, wrong?"

"You know perfectly well. You've got into the shit. Looks
to me like I've been away too long, huh?"

"No. It's nothing to do with you."

"I think it is. Don't you remember what I told you?
We've got the chance to do whatever we like. You don't
seem to've taken much notice. So spit it out, what's all that
rubbish you wrote to me?"

I tried to explain everything. About Morken and his
bullying and playing soldiers and the drivel about a hero's
death and the other stuff that led to me getting out of the HJ.

"I'm just not like you," I said to him. "I don't want
anything to do with people like that. They get on my
nerves."

He looked thoughtfully at me. Then we went into
our old bedroom, which we shared before he went away to
Sonthofen, and we sat on the bed.

"You remember who always came to your rescue when
you got beaten up in the street?" he asked.

"Yes. You."

"And who told you what was what when the old man
wouldn't open his mouth, yet again?"

"You again, dammit. But that's not fair, Horst. It's
got nothing to do with this."

"It has so got something to do with it. It's got a load to do with it. Because it means I expect you to listen to me—after everything I've done for you. Now that the old man's gone. So listen up! I know there are idiots in the HJ. Not everything works the way it should. But those are growing pains. You can't just run away when something like that happens. Just shut your eyes and get through it. How often d'you think I've had to do that?! Or do you think everything's just dropped into my lap these last few years?"

"No."

"There, you see. What are you thinking? D'you want to spend your whole life stuck in some crappy factory—like the old man? I'll tell you this, you *are* like me. Anything I can do, you can do too. So pull yourself together, kid, dammit!"

"Oh, pull myself together!" I said. "It's too late for that, it's done. Even if I wanted to, I couldn't go back."

"Nonsense! That's stupid talk, kid! Course you can go back. If I talk to them at the HJ, it'll be sorted. And not much fuss. You wouldn't have to crawl in the slush or anything like that. I might even be able to stop any bullying from any Morkens. I've got a lot of influence now, you know. And I'd use it for you. You just have to say the word."

"Yes, but that's just it," I said, and then I really did spill the beans. "It's not actually about Morken and all that stuff any more. I just don't like that whole direction, Horst."

He looked at me like he couldn't believe what he was hearing. "What the hell, have you completely flipped or what?" Then he grabbed my shoulders. "Who's putting stuff like that in your head? Who are these types you're hanging around with? Come on, tell me!"

"No. I can't tell you."

"What's that supposed to mean, you can't?" He gripped me harder. "Don't make me angry, kid!"

"We swore not to tell. They're my friends, Horst. Like the ones you had at that school. You remember? You told me about it."

He hesitated but then he let me go. Friendship and comradeship was definitely the right tack to take with him. After a while he nodded.

"All right, you don't want to rat on your friends. Fine, I won't force you. No need. I'll find it all out, believe me."

When he said that, I was scared that the things he found out would get us in trouble. I wanted to stop him. But he cut me off.

"Don't tell me what to do, squirt," he said. "There's no way I'm watching you ruin everything. If you won't look out for yourself, I'll have to." He stood up and walked to the door, but then turned back again. "There's this lad in charge of you lot, isn't there? What does he call himself? Flint?"

Then I felt sick. "Where did you hear that?" I stammered.

"Asked around about you a bit. What's the fella's real name then?"

"No idea."

"So you don't want to say? Doesn't matter either way. I'll find him. And when I'm done with him, he'll leave you in peace. You can bet your life on that."

With that, he was gone. I called after him because I didn't want him to go for Flint. But there was no talking to him. He's always been like that. When Horst gets an idea in his head, he acts on it. And I couldn't blame him this time. After all, he thinks he's doing it for me.

Now I'm sitting here and I don't know if I should warn Flint. Or what I should do. Cos one thing's for sure: if those two meet, it'll be a disaster. And a mighty big one!

18th April 1943

I don't know how Horst managed it, but he tracked Flint down somehow. They went somewhere nobody'd bother them and sorted things out between them. After that, Horst came back home. He looked like a steam train had run over his face. All red and swollen, cut and bruised. But he wasn't all that bothered by it: no, he was in a great mood.

"I showed that bastard," he announced, almost before he'd come through the door.

"He's not a bastard, Horst. He's my friend. What did you do to him?"

"Ha, what I said I would, what else? I *made it clear* that he's to leave you alone. And I had a couple of damn convincing arguments." He whacked his fist into his hand. "Think he got it. Came off a bit worse than I *did*, you see."

"You're off your rocker. Stop barging in! I *didn't* ask you to..."

"I'll barge in as much as I like. You've proved you're not capable of managing your own affairs. So I'll do it for you. No reason to get worked up!"

Then he came over and put his hand on my shoulder. "And now, listen up! There's no problem about the HJ—I spoke to a few people this morning. You can go back any time just as if nothing happened. Same for Tom. So get down to business tomorrow. But you'll have to do it without me—I can't come and hold your hand this time. I've got to go, duty calls!"

"Horst, I don't know if..."

"But I do. Next time I come, this'll all be sorted. Got that?"

"How long will you be away?"

"D'you think they tell us that? There's loads to do. Might be a while before I have a day or two free."

"And where are you going?"

"Somewhere in the east. I'll find out tomorrow once we're on the way. But even if I knew, I wouldn't be allowed to talk about it."

"What will you have to do, then?"

"Don't know, kid. Now stop asking questions! Just get yourself back on track! I don't want to hear any more complaints about you, see?"

After that, he said goodbye to me and Mum. I went out for a walk. Suddenly I felt unsure again. I felt small and ridiculous after everything Horst had said. Maybe I really am getting it all wrong, I thought. And he's done so much for me! I can't disappoint him now!

Later in the evening, I met the others. Flint was the last to arrive. He looked pretty much the same as Horst. No big difference. And he was on equally top form.

"Hey, Gerlo," he said. "Your bastard of a brother came to see me today."

"He's not a bastard, he's just my brother, yeah? Let's leave it there, Flint."

"Fine, whatever. He wanted me to leave you alone. Did you know about that?"

"He told me. What happened?"

"That's between him and me. Anyway, I made it clear to him that you're one of us, and not one of those idiots at the HJ. So that's cleared up once and for all."

"Funny. The way he tells it is a bit different."

Flint laughed. "If he wants me to beat it into his head, he's more than welcome. I'm always ready to hear from him. Tell him that!"

"Can't. His term of duty starts tomorrow."

"What kind of duty?"

"In the SS."

When Flint heard that, his mood dropped like a stone. He came over and sat down beside me. "Now, listen up, Gerlo. Maybe he's your brother and means a lot to you. But from now on you've got to be careful with him. I mean, SS, man! They get it drilled into them to report everything. Family means nothing to them in the end."

"Yeah, I know. But Horst's different."

"C'mon, don't tell yourself that rubbish, man. He was at that Nazi school for years, wasn't he? So he isn't different. Even if he used to be—they twist everyone. You can't tell him a thing about us—not ever! No matter what!"

"Hey, Flint, I never told him anything and I never will. What d'you take me for? D'you want to kick me out?"

"No." He held up his hand and shook his head. "No, I don't. Sorry, man." That was the first time I ever heard him apologize for anything. "I want you to stay. You're one of us. Nobody can change that."

Later, we all sat around together, messing about. Course, Flint's face was the main talking point, cos it'd gone all the colours of the rainbow by then. We sang our songs and talked about everything we want to do in the next little while. After that, I knew more than ever: I'm never going back to the HJ! The Edelweiss Pirates are the best friends I've ever had. I belong to them and no one else. Like Flint said.

I'm not angry with Horst for trying to get me back on the right track—on his right track, that is. I'd even be sad if he didn't, cos then I'd think he didn't care about me any more. But I won't do what he wants. I am different from him. Eventually he'll see that.

In a way, my visits to old Mr Gerlach were like excursions into another world. In his room, everything was quiet and peaceful, everything happened slowly and carefully—and that was pretty much the opposite of what I was used to in my own life. He was always quiet and reserved too; in all that time, I never heard him raise his voice. He seemed very gentle to me and it was hard to imagine him ever hurting another person.

So I was all the more astonished by what I read in his diary. All the rebelliousness and slang, the fights and battles with the HJ: it just didn't fit. The casual way that he and his friends slipped on the knuckledusters and got into fights—I couldn't reconcile it with him. One day, I asked him about it.

"So, that surprises you?" he said.

"Yes, it does somehow. Things get a bit wild with me and my mates sometimes—but not like that. And it really doesn't fit with you!"

"Oh! You think so?" He looked at me in amazement, then nodded. "Well, yes, you didn't live through it. You can't imagine what things were like back then. Beatings and fights were just normal. They were part of everyday life; we didn't even think about it. My father, for example, he thrashed me all the time."

"Why? Did he drink?"

"No, not really. Not more than anyone else, anyway. I don't know why he did it. Probably because that's how his father treated him. He didn't know anything else; it was just how things were. He wouldn't even have understood if you'd asked him about it. Words didn't get you very far in our neck of the woods, you know. If there was a dispute, you didn't talk, you hit out. That's just what it was like."

He stood up and shut the balcony door. Outside, it had started to snow, an icy wind was blowing. I'd noticed before, on my last visit, that the cold took it out of him, even if he tried not to show it.

"It was the same everywhere," he continued, once he'd sat back down. "At school, the teachers beat us; in the HJ, the leaders beat us; and our instructors beat us at work. We didn't need to do anything—they always found a reason. And besides: there was a war on. The soldiers got bravery medals for killing. Everyone loved them for their heroism. There was violence wherever you looked. We grew up with it."

He waved a hand. It was rare for him to use so many words, the speech seemed to have exhausted him. When he stood up, he looked tired. He went over to the window, where the birdcage stood. Then he reached for the packet of seed.

"Don't get the wrong impression," he said. "We weren't hardened criminals or anything like that. But we didn't avoid fights either. The things we experienced built up so much rage in us that it needed a way out. And that was easiest with our fists."

I watched him feed the birds. They were his pride and joy. Now and then, he let them out of the cage, and they flew around the room and walked up and down on the cupboard. When he whistled, they came back and perched on his finger. His favourite game was to breathe on them. Then they shook themselves, ruffled their feathers and puffed themselves up.

He always seemed lost in thought when he did that. I liked to watch. He looked so peaceful.

14th June 1943

*After things went so smoothly the first time, we've had
another couple of goes at delivering leaflets in the last few
weeks. So that people wouldn't think it had all just been a
silly joke. So they'd see there's a system. That we mean it.*

*For a long time, nothing bad happened. We were
always careful, nobody caught us or trailed us. But, of
course, we couldn't see what was going on behind the scenes.
And there must have been loads happening. As we found
out for ourselves, last night.*

*Like every year, it was time for our Whitsun outing to
the Felsensee and yesterday morning we set off. Everything
went fine at first. We were prepared, so it wouldn't be like
last year when we got nabbed by the SS at the station. Flint
had got hold of fake travel passes for inspection. And we
wore plain clothes with our real stuff in our rucksacks till
we got to the Felsensee. So we'd attract less attention, or so
we hoped—apart from our hair. But we left that as it is.
We're not quite that careful yet!*

*There were at least twice as many people at the lake
as last year. Easily a couple of hundred. We know almost
everyone by now. When we walked down the path, they
greeted us with a storm of applause and no end of fuss.
Almost like we'd been away from home for a year and just*

got back. The best moment is always when we step out of the trees and there's the sun and the smell of fire and the glittering water, and there are the others, and we know: now we're back where we belong and where no one can touch us. Where everyone's on our side. Where we can be totally our real selves.

Over the day, we heard that the Wuppertalers who we sat with last year, and a few other groups, have been through some bad stuff recently. They didn't exactly want to talk about it, but in the evening, round the fire, they did tell us.

"Our local slammer is really brutal," one of them said. The one who warned us about the SS last year. "That's why a few of us aren't here this year. Banged up in there, waiting for their trials."

Course, that really made us pay attention. We wanted to know what had happened. He looked round the ring, like he wanted to check everyone sitting round the fire could be trusted. Then he started to talk.

"Last November, we went on a weekend to Düsseldorf, to meet a few folks there. Someone must've grassed. Any rate, suddenly the SS were there, and they collared us. Frisked us at the cop shop. Stupidly we had a few leaflets on us, which we'd been taking to the Düsseldorfers. So anyway, there was a massive fuss, you can imagine. They took us to the Gestapo right away."

When he said that, all at once it was dead silent. We're used to a thing or two these days and it's not that easy to

shock us. But—Gestapo! That's a word that sends chills
down your spine. A word you only whisper. And you hope
never to have anything to do with them.

"And then?" Floss asked eventually.

He looked at her briefly. Then he shook his head and
stared into the fire. "Don't want to talk about it," he
muttered.

Somehow, that was worse than if he'd reeled off a
never-ending description of hell. Normally, we don't admit
it if something scares us. You skim over it with a few jokes
or talk like it doesn't bother you.

What must have happened to him! I thought. It must
be bad if even that guy, who's always so cool, can't talk
about it!

"It set off a whole avalanche," another Wuppertaler
said. "They searched hundreds of flats. Round our way,
in Düsseldorf, Duisburg, Essen—kept widening the circle.
Confiscated anything that wasn't nailed down. Fake travel
permits, guitars, songs, letters, clothes, Edelweiss badges—
everything. Anywhere they found anything bad—leaflets
or weapons—they nicked people. They're the ones going on
trial."

"If they're found guilty," Flint asked, "what'll happen
then?"

"If they're lucky, jail. If not, it'll be Moringen. The
youth concentration camp."

He told us other stuff too, and hammered it into us to
be damn careful with everything. No names, don't leave

addresses lying around, don't write down any songs or anything else. Nobody's safe any more, he said. Since the business with the leaflets.

"Where did you get them from anyway?" Lanky asked.

"At first we used the British ones and sent them out secretly. But then they didn't drop any for ages. So we started to make our own. One said: 'Soon will come the day, when we're free again. When we cast off every chain. When there's no more need to hide, the songs we sing inside.' We mostly dropped them in places where there are loads of people. Stations and so on. Then we scarpered. Cos if you got caught—oh boy! It'd be the Gestapo for you. And if they get their hands on you, God help you!"

That evening we were deep in thought as we settled down to sleep. It had started to rain, so we'd crawled into our tents. Eventually we dropped off, but a sound woke us in the middle of the night. I didn't know what was happening at first. I only saw that the door of our tent was open, that there were people there in these heavy black boots and there was some kind of water trickling in on us. Then Flint started yelling and it dawned on me: the people standing there were SS men and they were pissing on us.

We wanted to storm out. But before we could, the tent was slit open from all sides. Someone dragged me out and I got a whack on the head that made me think it'd been broken into a thousand pieces. When my head had almost stopped spinning, I saw that a massive troop of the SS had attacked the camp. They must have overpowered the lookouts. They were at every tent, pulling people out and beating them. Going berserk, hitting out with clubs and iron bars. No one had a chance to defend themselves cos everyone was still half asleep and behind them were guys with sub-machine guns, pointed at us.

There was blood running down my face and I lay still on the ground so no one would get the idea of lamming me again. It was hell having to watch the thrashing without being able to do anything. But what choice did I have? There were just too many of them, they were armed, and wouldn't stop at anything.

Eventually it was over. They dragged us up and drove us to the shore. Flint and Knuckles were the worst off of our group cos they'd fought back longest. But the rest of us didn't look much better. Everyone was bleeding, Ferret could hardly walk. Only the girls had been left alone—at least that's what it looked like.

Then they led us away. Up the path and down to the Rhine. We were still in total shock, trotted along like a bunch of convicts. They kept yelling and whacking us on our backs. There were lorries down on the road. We had to tell them our city, then they put us on the right lorry. They put the tarps down and we set off for Cologne—or Wuppertal, or wherever.

It was a spookily quiet journey. Nobody dared say anything or look at anyone in case they hit us again. Eventually the lorry stopped, we were pushed out and taken to a building. When I saw it, my heart sank to my boots,

*and I bet everyone was the same. It was the EL-DE House,
on Appellhofplatz. The Cologne Gestapo HQ—anyone with
a brain steers well clear.*

*It was the middle of the night, but all the windows were
brightly lit. They seemed to be expecting us. We had to go in
and stand in a line along the wall in a long, bare corridor.
It was a bit like last year at the police station—but worse.
There's something in the air in that place that does you in.
And then there are all the stories! Screams that you can
hear out in the street in the middle of the night. Couldn't
help remembering them as I stood there. I was shaking I
was so scared.*

*I was at the front of the queue so I had to go in first.
The room they took me to was quite small and there was
a funny kind of smell in there. Two Gestapo men were
waiting for me. One was small and thin and was sitting at
a desk when I came in. The other was tall and strong, with
an ugly, brutal face. He was leaning on the wall.*

*First they took my details. The thin one asked the ques-
tions and wrote everything down on some form. Weirdly, he
was very friendly and even cracked a joke now and then.
The ugly one didn't say a word. Just stood there, staring at
me from the side, his face never changing. Now and then
his hands twitched. That made me nervous.*

*The thin one asked why I'd been down at the Felsensee,
what my clothes meant, why I wasn't in the HJ, who I hang
round with here in Cologne and so on. Clearly wanted to
hear about the Edelweiss Pirates. I acted dumb, like last*

year with the police. But I had a bad feeling from the start.
Cos one thing was clear: all three of us knew I was lying.

Eventually, the thin one stood up and walked round the
table. "Come along now, my boy," he said, laying a hand
on my shoulder. "Out with it now, why did you do it? The
leaflets, I mean?"

I was taken totally by surprise. How the hell did he
know that? I thought. Nobody had ever seen us. Or had
they? Maybe someone had been spying on us? One of the
block wardens? And dished the dirt on us?

Luckily, I got my act together right at the last second
before I said anything stupid. No! I thought. They don't
know anything. They can't know anything. Course they
heard about the leaflets. Probably found some in their own
letter boxes. And now they want to know who it was. We're
from Ehrenfeld and we've already been in trouble with the
police. So we're suspects. And now they're trying the old
trick of pretending they already know everything.

So I asked, "What leaflets?"

But almost the moment I said it, the ugly one was on
me. So fast I didn't even see him coming. He grabbed me,
one hand on my collar, the other in my hair, and pushed me
into the desk.

"The-leaf-lets-that-were-in-the-let-ter-box-es-in-Eh-ren-
feld," he roared, slamming my head into the tabletop with
every syllable.

The cut on my forehead from the Felsensee opened
up again, blood dripped onto the table. My head almost

burst, I felt dizzy. I had to hold on tight, or I'd have keeled over.

The thin one pulled the ugly one off me, took him to one side and ticked him off. Told him to calm down, etc. Then he came back to me and held out a handkerchief.

"Here, clean up your face."

I took the hankie and pressed it to my head to stop the bleeding.

"And clean that mess off the desk while you're at it—and quick about it!" the ugly one roared from the side.

I tried to do what he said, but it didn't work. Whenever I took the hankie off my forehead to clean the desk, it dripped again. I couldn't keep up with the fresh blood.

The ugly one kept working himself up more and more. Saying I'd owe them a new desk if I didn't clean this one up. The thin one ticked him off again. Then he gave me a second hankie and that worked. I pressed the old one on my head and wiped the table with the new one till there was no more blood.

"Good," the thin one said. "You're doing well. Now, do you want to tell us anything about the leaflets?"

"But I really don't know anything!"

The ugly one wanted to let rip again, but the thin one held him back.

"You're deep in the shit, lad," he said. "But I want to help you. You just have to meet me halfway. Otherwise, I'll be forced to leave you alone with my colleague. Got that?"

"But it's true. We're not interested in leaflets or any of that. Yeah, we sometimes do silly things. But we just want a bit of fun. We don't give a monkey's about politics and all that. It's over our heads."

They kept pumping me for some time but by then I was sure they didn't have anything on us, or they'd have come out with it long ago. So I stuck to my story that we were harmless. I don't know if they ended up believing it or just didn't know what else to do. Anyway, they let me go. But first they said I wouldn't get off so lightly next time. If I got into trouble again, then they'd keep me there and put me through the wringer or send me to a military training camp or come up with something else. Any rate, I should keep clear of them.

Course I made damn sure I got away ASAP. Then I managed to get home somehow to lick my wounds.

Today I met the others. They'd all had about the same treatment. Except the thin one had said I'd already confessed to everything so there was no point in denying it. But luckily no one fell for it. No one told them anything, everyone played dumb. Looks like we got away with a scare and a few bumps and bruises.

Course, we're in a lousy mood. Wasn't how we'd imagined our Whitsun trip. Now we're not even safe at the Felsensee. And from now on, probably any time anything happens in Ehrenfeld, we'll have the Gestapo breathing down our necks. Not exactly a rosy future!

But there's something else sitting like a stone in my belly. When they took me into the EL-DE House for *questioning, I passed some stairs down to the cellar. And I heard something down there. Terrible screams, like animals.*

But it wasn't animals. It was people screaming down there.

29th June 1943

After that happened with the Gestapo, we kept our heads down for a while. None of us wanted to admit it, but we were really frightened by the whole business. Although it had turned out all right in the end, we somehow couldn't shake off the feeling that the torturers in the EL-DE House were capable of a lot more than that. Any rate, none of us is all that keen on meeting them again.

So we left the leaflets alone for a bit and didn't meet up for a while either. It wasn't till last night that we got together again—and even that was kind of forced on us. Cos the sirens went off in the middle of the night: air raid. I snatched the case that Mum keeps ready by the bed. Then I grabbed her and took her off to the Taku bunker. Outside it was almost as bright as day from the searchlights in the sky and the parachute flares dropped by the planes. The flak was going off like mad and the air was full of clattering shrapnel, which rained down on us. And just as we got to the bunker, the first bombs dropped.

Mum went in and down while I waited for the others. Bit by bit, they all arrived. We really wanted to stay outside

like we always do, but last night was too hot even for us.
It wasn't just a raid, more like halfway to the end of the
world. A hundred times worse than the thousand-bomber
raid last year. Ended up with so much smoke and dust in
the air we could hardly breathe and couldn't see a thing, so
we did go down into the bunker after all.

The air raid warden wanted to show us to our places.
But we acted like he wasn't there and sat where we liked.
The mood down there was like a nightmare. Everyone
crouched in their chairs, suitcases between their legs, gas
masks in their laps, waiting to see what was coming. A
couple of hits were so near the plaster trickled down off
the ceiling. Once the power went off. It was pitch black,
everyone shrieked, the warden shouted a bit and acted
important. But after a few minutes, the light came on
again and eventually, the worst was over. The noise stopped
and we got ourselves out of that hole.

Everyone wanted to know how things were at home, so
we split up. Me and Tom waited for our mums and went
back to Klarastrasse with them. Not much had happened to
our block but a couple of other buildings nearby were on fire
or reduced to rubble. We went over and tried to help. What
we saw was awful. In one place, the cellar where people had
been sheltering was buried. We could hear them screaming.
We tried to clear the rubble and dig down to them. But it
was hopeless. Half the building was on top of them. It got to
a point where we couldn't do another thing and had to give
up. The cries had stopped ages ago by then.

145

People kept wandering by, right out of their minds.
Covered in blood and dirt, calling out for people, their
kids or whoever. And then there were more attacks. Cluster
bombs and aerial mines now, in the middle of the burn-
ing streets. We had to take cover every minute or two. All
around us were dead bodies in the rubble.

Today I went out with Flint and Tom to see what
was left of Ehrenfeld. Not much, half the town's in ruins.
There were forced labourers digging out the bodies and,
on every street, you could see bombed-out people loading
their worldly goods onto some kind of cart and taking them
away. Most of them didn't know where they were going.

"I'm telling you, there was a method to the cluster
bombs," said Flint. "They chucked 'em down once everyone
was out helping. Wanted to do in as many people as pos-
sible, believe you me."

"But why?" Tom shook his head. "I don't understand.
It wasn't poor sods like us in Ehrenfeld who started the war,
but the top Nazis in Berlin. Why don't the British stick it to
them?"

"Oh, stop dreaming," Flint said. "The top brass are all
the same. Whatever country they're from."

As we walked on, we saw that the HJ had been busy.
They'd run around everywhere with buckets of paint and
splashed morale-boosting slogans on the walls. Stuff like
"The final victory is ours!" Or "The German People don't
give up!" We didn't know whether to laugh or cry, we
found it so sick.

Eventually, Flint stopped by one of the slogans. "The fight goes on!" it said on the wall. He pointed at it and looked at us.

"What d'you reckon, people?" he said. "Is that meant as a challenge?"

31st July 1943

Didn't take long for us to put the slogan on the wall into action. A few days after the raid, we met up in the Volksgarten, and actually we agreed pretty quickly: we can't let ourselves get thrown off course just cos the Gestapo grilled us a bit! After all, nothing happened apart from a few bloody noses. And if we're careful, it can stay that way.

Besides, when we thought about the day in the EL-DE House, we were filled with a cold rage. "We can't just take that lying down," Lanky said. "We've got to do something, got to show them. We owe it to ourselves."

"Yes," Flint said. "And anyway, our lives aren't worth a damn any more, if the raids keep on like that. So there's no need to go over the top in being careful."

We remembered what the Wuppertalers had told us at the Felsensee about their leaflets, and decided to copy them. Lanky reckoned he knew someone who worked as an apprentice printer. Said he thought like us and could keep a secret, so he'd ask him about helping us.

A few days later, Lanky had arranged things. Didn't say the chap's name, just that we could trust him. We didn't ask. Sometimes it's better not to know stuff. If I was him, I'd insist on it.

About two or three weeks ago, the first leaflets were ready, and now we've got several with different messages. We never write much cos people don't want to read a whole novel. Usually just a headline like "Down with the Nazis" or "Stop the War", and then we explain that all the propaganda is lies and say stuff about how things really are.

Most of the time it's Floss and Lanky who do the texts, they're best at it. But when it comes to giving them out, Flint's in charge. He's in his element and has a new idea every time for how to do it. The first time, we hid the leaflets in the station bogs cos people there have most time for reading and no worries about being seen. The second time, we went into the churches and slipped them into the hymn books. Next time, Flint wants to come up with a way for smuggling them into factory canteens.

We haven't done the letter boxes in Ehrenfeld again. Too risky. They'd suspect us at once and drag us off to the EL-DE House. And who knows what methods they'd come up with then! We never write anything on the leaflets to show who they're by. Lanky once suggested putting an edelweiss flower on them but we soon ditched that idea. Much too dangerous! Besides, as Floss said, let people wonder who's behind it—it won't do them any harm.

Sometimes I wonder what happens to the leaflets and if they ever have any effect. But Flint reckons there's no point asking. 1) We'll never find out. And 2) none of the big stuff in history would've happened if people had started by worrying about whether there was any point. Just get on with things without thinking too much about them, he said, that's what counts.

22nd August 1943

So now we know what we are: a band of criminals. A "growth on the body of the nation that must be burnt out and destroyed". That's what it said in the newspaper— Lanky read it. Anyway, that's how far we've gone now.

It was Flint's idea. About two weeks ago. "We ought to do something really big," he said. "Not just hiding leaflets in the bogs! Let's climb the dome at the central station and rain them down on people from there. If it works, the whole of Cologne'll be talking about it."

At first we thought he'd flipped. But he was so excited by the idea and kept on about it for so long that he talked us into going down to the station to have a recce. He'd already been down there himself and planned it all out. He'd do the most dangerous part himself—climbing up with the leaflets—he explained. The rest of us should keep a lookout in case the cops turned up. We'd need one of us in each corner of the main hall and two of us in the middle—so right underneath him—disguised as a courting couple. The advantage of that was that they could see in all directions without attracting attention. If they stayed cuddled up it would mean all-clear. But as soon as they moved apart and started arguing, he'd have to take cover. That way they could warn him without immediately giving the game away.

The plan didn't sound bad but when we looked up into the dome, we still felt a bit sick. I thought, isn't this biting off a bit more than we can chew? The others had a few doubts too. But Flint was sure it'd work and cos Knuckles and Lanky were on his side, in the end we decided to go ahead.

We spent several days getting everything ready. Got the leaflets printed and hid them in the ruins of an old church. Then we spent as much time as we could hanging around the station to work out the best time for our plan and where we'd need to stand to keep everything in sight.

So yesterday was the day. We reckoned Tom and Floss would make the best lovers. Specially cos they've actually been a couple for a few weeks now. Flint reckoned they'd have the advantage of not having to pretend. They could just do what they do all the time anyway. He grinned at me and I knew what he meant. Since Floss hooked up with Tom, you can't do a thing with the guy.

But then, the day before the action, Floss got sick. For a moment we thought about chucking it all in, but then we stuck to it cos we'd got everything so well planned and didn't want to leave the leaflets hanging around for longer than we had to. So Tilly said she'd stand in for Floss. Tom reckoned that was OK but he still had the wind up a bit in case Floss got jealous of him fooling around with Tilly on the platform, even if it was only acting. So he asked if I'd take over. I said, sure, why not? Don't want you getting into trouble! And so we had a new couple.

At the station, we posted ourselves where we'd discussed. Ferret, Maja, Goethe and Tom stood in the four corners of the big hall. We kept Knuckles and Lanky back as a kind of rapid reaction force, just in case. Tilly and me went into the centre of the hall, under the dome. And Flint set off with the leaflets, which were hidden in an old work bag.

There are iron staples on one of the pillars—for the workmen if anything needs fixing up in the roof. Flint was going to climb them, and he was dressed as a workman too so he wouldn't stand out. While he climbed, me and Tilly started cuddling. That meant I could watch half the hall—where Tom and Goethe were—and Tilly could see the other half with Maja and Ferret. It was heaving, like it always is on Saturdays. Trains coming in and out all the time and people everywhere, hurrying this way and that way and almost running into each other.

We'd agreed with Flint that Tilly and I would start kissing when we were sure it was all clear. That would be his sign to climb up into the rafters. We didn't see anything suspicious and everyone else in the corners was calm too, so we started. And that's when it happened. I've known for

151

ages that I'm quite keen on Tilly. But I had no idea she was interested in me. Seems that was a mistake. Anyway, she suddenly kissed me like the Last Judgement was just around the corner. I didn't know which way was up, I was so bowled over. We forgot everything around us. Stupidly, we also forgot our promise to look out for Flint.

So we didn't see the police patrol coming through the hall. Tom and Goethe must have been waving like mad— or they said they were later—but I didn't notice. Somehow Tilly spotted Ferret and just about rescued it in time. Before I knew what was happening, she pulled away from me and started shouting: what was I thinking of, jumping on her like that? In broad daylight! In front of all these people!

It was only then I saw the police. They came over and asked Tilly if I was bothering her. She shook her head and said, no, I wasn't. It was just that sometimes in the heat of the moment I went too far and forgot myself. But that was all, they didn't need to worry.

Luckily they walked on—and didn't look up. Tilly and me carried on arguing till they were out of sight. Then we gradually started canoodling again to show Flint he could carry on. I wished I could glance up at him cos I wanted to know if everything was all right but we'd agreed never to do that—whatever happened. So as not to give anyone the idea anything might be going on up there.

But there were no more incidents and after a bit we saw Flint climbing down again. He nodded to us and we

all walked to the steps—one by one so as not to stand out.
He must've done something to make the leaflets float down
a bit later—not right away. Me and Tilly had just got
to the steps when it started. Everyone stopped and stared
up like they couldn't believe their eyes. We beat it. Cos we
knew it wouldn't be long till that place was crawling with
police—and worse.

Anyway, Flint was right: today, all Cologne is talking
about it. The Gestapo are probably already questioning
people who were at the station at that time. I just hope
nobody remembers us. Flint climbing the staples. Or a
young couple acting funny.

Talking of couples... I'm meeting Tilly in a bit—without the others. But first I'll go and see Floss and take her
some flowers. As a little thank you. For getting sick.

In the days after Christmas, I made my last visits to old Mr Gerlach in his flat, even though I had no idea of that at the time. Although I could tell that he wasn't particularly well, we never talked about it and I didn't worry too much about it.

When I walked down a road in those days, I often found myself comparing the things I could see there with what he'd written in his diary. There were a few times when—involuntarily, almost as if my feet had carried me there by themselves—I found myself in places that played a role in his story. And every time it happened, I lingered there, stumped. I kept coming up against a surface busyness with no trace of the things I'd read about. It almost seemed like time had wiped everything away—completely and irretrievably.

"Why did you do it?" I asked the old man on one of my visits. "You and your friends? Why did you rebel when everyone else kept quiet?"

"Oh, now, you mustn't get the wrong idea," he said. "We were no heroes. We didn't go and stand in the streets yelling, 'Join us, let's free our country, let's fight against tyranny!' We were perfectly ordinary young people who just wanted our freedom. But it was extra important to us, somehow. Perhaps that was what made us different from the others:

we were hooked on our own very personal freedom. And we were determined to fight anyone who denied it to us."

Whenever he spoke like that, there was a change in him. Then he didn't appear like an old man any more, and even his cough seemed to disappear. And something suddenly became clear to me: that word "freedom", which was so very important to him, meant nothing to me. I could have defined it, of course—I could have written a ten-page essay on the subject. But I didn't have an emotional connection to it like he did.

He seemed to feel what was going on inside me. "Perhaps you can't understand that," he said. "You have every possible freedom these days. You kids can do or not do what you want—well, within reason anyway. But then it was different. Everything was regimented. Even at fourteen, we had to work ten-, twelve-hour days in the factories, six days a week. And the rest of the time, we were ordered about in the Hitler Youth and prepared for war. We just wanted to shake off those limits and make our dreams of a free life a reality—no matter how."

"And the Nazis were in your way?"

"Yes," he said. "We didn't know much about politics and that kind of thing, and we weren't particularly interested in them—at least at first. OK, we knew that we couldn't stand the Nazis, but that was just a feeling, we couldn't have explained it properly. We just fell into the whole thing. The situation escalated even though we didn't really want that."

"So if the Nazis had left you alone, you wouldn't have done any of it?"

He shrugged. "Quite possibly," he said in the end. "I don't know. At any rate, they didn't leave us alone. They couldn't stand it if anyone lived or thought differently from their ideas of what was correct. So they persecuted us and fought us. First the Hitler Youth, then the police, then the SS and finally the Gestapo. It got worse and worse, and more and more brutal. Except," he looked at me and smiled, "we were really pig-headed. So they achieved the opposite of what they wanted. They drove us really wild. Whatever they did, it just made us want to give them a taste of their own medicine. And so we turned the tables—and started fighting them."

He pointed out through the window. "We didn't know where it would all lead, didn't think much about it. We didn't have a plan or anything like that either. It all happened spontaneously, depending on how we felt. We really just went with our gut instincts. We knew that somehow we'd end up on the right side then."

When I left the home that day, I took a detour through the Volksgarten. It was freezing cold but the sun was shining and there, where the snow was undisturbed, it scrunched under my shoes. I stopped in the middle of the park and looked around. I wondered what was still here from back then. Was there such a thing as a memory in the trees or in the walls? Was anything written into things?

Would they set it free if you asked them?

26th January 1944

*We haven't had a winter like this for years now. Nothing
but bitter cold for weeks and it doesn't look like getting
better any time soon. There's practically no coal anywhere.
We're only heating one room here at home and the others
are mostly doing the same. Luckily there's Tilly. We take
turns to sleep at hers and mine. The room might be cold
but we keep ourselves warm under the covers one way or
another.*

*But it's not just the cold that's getting on our nerves.
People hardly have a crust to eat now. The rations are
getting shorter and shorter. People would almost beat each
other's heads in for a decent lump of meat. There's still half
a pound of bread per day for everyone but—well, they call
it bread. No idea what they put in it. Sawdust and old
leaves probably. Nothing that'll fill you up, anyway.*

*So most people get supplies on the black market. Nobody
talks about it much cos it's illegal. "Sabotage of provision
for the German nation"—such a nice phrase. But no one
cares about slogans, your belly is more important to you
than the German nation. So nobody feels guilty about it,
certainly not here in Ehrenfeld.*

*Of us lot, Flint and Knuckles know their way round
the black market best. They're eighteen now. Knuckles's*

birthday was two weeks ago, and Flint's not long after. So they half expect to be conscripted and sent to the front any day now. They're officially exempt, cos their work is vital for the war. But that could change any time if their bosses don't like their faces—then they'd be fair game.

Course they won't let that happen. We've all sworn that none of us will go to war and shoot at strangers who've never done us any harm. If they get called up, Flint says, they'll go underground. And make damn sure nobody finds them. Except they'd need something to live on. So it's useful for them to know a bit about how to get on with the black market. Cos then they wouldn't have any other way of earning money.

They've had their first go at it now. Flint told me about it a day or two back. I was speechless, it was all so new to me.

"What can you get then?" I asked.

"Oh, you know, anything you need. Fancy a piece of juicy roast venison? No problem, it'll cost you a watch. Or a fat Christmas goose? Cough up a few trinkets from your jewellery box and it's yours. Why would you hang onto it? Junk like that's useless anyway, we'll all be six feet under soon."

"But—where does the stuff come from? I mean, venison! There's been none of that for years."

"Wrong! It's been there. But not for the little people. Just for the big shots."

"And how does it all work?"

"Same as ever. With the war on, there are loads of corrupt junior officials keen to make a bit on the side. So they siphon off some of the stuff they look after and sell it themselves. Just enough that nobody notices. The big fish in the pond snap the stuff up—they're raking it in. In comparison with them, folks like Knuckles and me who occasionally hand a bit on from them to the little people aren't worth mentioning."

"But—those big fish, how come they don't get rumbled? If they're so deep in this business, someone ought to've caught them by now!"

Flint grinned. "Course. Everyone knows who they are. If the Nazis wanted, they could bust them, one by one. But they don't want. They're not stupid, those guys. They keep the party high-ups supplied with everything they need. For free, of course. And only the best! So they get protected in return. You scratch my back, I'll scratch yours!"

"You mean, the propaganda—sabotage and all that..."

"Only applies to the little people, not the big beasts. And certainly not to them in the Party. Don't kid yourself, Gerlo. Wherever you look, this place stinks! To high heaven!"

He told me more, and when I heard it, I thought, well, if that's how it is—then grub's up! I suspect that Mum's secretly starving herself so I get enough to eat and honestly, the thought goes against my sense of honour. I've talked to Tom so I know his mum's doing the same. So we'll order a few decent things from Flint and Knuckles next time, so we can get a bit of meat on our bones again.

This isn't the time to hang back, we decided. After all, we're meant to take the Führer as our example!

19th February 1944

Who'da thought it! People act like they don't care and their faces are dead, but behind all that there are still a few brave souls who dare take a chance—at least here in Ehrenfeld. And that was a damn good thing last night. Daren't think what might've happened to me and Tilly otherwise.

After our efforts at the station last summer, all hell broke loose for a bit. The Nazis threw everything at finding out who it was. We kept our heads down for ages, to be on the safe side, and luckily they didn't get to thinking of us. They probably don't reckon we're capable of something on that scale and suspect it must've been the communists or British spies or something.

When we realized they had nothing on us, we put our feelers out again and carried on. There were a few leaflet campaigns in the autumn, but nothing so big—too risky for the time being. And in the winter—when it got so cold that nobody with any sense would set foot outside—we started going out at night and painting slogans on the walls. Wherever we knew lots of people would walk past *in the morning. Flint and Knuckles started it, and when nothing happened to them, the rest of us copied. Tom and Floss had their first go a couple of weeks ago, and then Tilly and me plucked up our courage.*

Last night we were out again. We'd picked a railway underpass. 1) Cos loads of people have to walk to work that way in the mornings. And 2) cos it's harder to see you if anyone is out in the streets after all. But there was one thing we hadn't thought of—a place like that can easily turn into a trap that you can't escape.

I dunno if we were just unlucky or maybe we weren't careful enough. Anyway, we were in the middle of it, and had just painted the first words when a handful of SS men turned up at one end of the tunnel. They were in uniform but I don't reckon they were a proper patrol. Probably been out boozing. That's what it looked like, anyway.

When they saw us, they stopped and stared like they couldn't believe it. We immediately chucked away the bucket and brushes and scarpered as fast as we could. They roared after us to stop, and then chased us. Down the tunnel, their boots clanged like pistol shots. We ran like rabbits. Luckily there was no one at the other end or we'd have been done for. They would've finished us.

Out on the roads, it was slippery. Slush everywhere and in the dark we couldn't see where we were stepping. At first that seemed like an advantage cos them behind us were so drunk they could barely stay on their feet, and after a few minutes we'd almost shaken them off. But then Tilly slipped on a street corner and fell flat on her face. When she tried to stand up, she knew she was in a mess: sprained ankle! She could barely walk.

But it was no use, we had to go on. She leant on me and we limped off the best we could. Course then we were far too slow. No chance to get away like that: they were gaining on us. I was desperately trying to think what to do but had no ideas. We turned a corner and then Tilly was totally done in. She was groaning with pain.

I pulled her into the nearest backyard and we cowered against the wall, hoping the SS men would run past and not find us. But they weren't so obliging, probably saw our tracks in the snow. It was awful: we could hear them coming and couldn't do a thing. Not a single thing. There was no way out.

But just at that moment, a door opened, right behind us. Someone pulled us inside and shut the door again. We were standing in a hallway and in the dim light we could see that our guardian angel was two old folks. They pushed us on into their bedroom, and opened a wardrobe and squeezed us in. Neither of them said a word. They closed the wardrobe door and locked it and we crouched in the dark holding our breath.

Right away there was a din. The SS were hammering on the doors, one flat after another, and yelling to let them in. Eventually they got to us. The pounding on the door went right through our bones. We heard them storm in and start searching the flat. Before long, they were in the

*bedroom. Tilly and me clung onto each other. I think one
already had his hand on the wardrobe door when the old
woman said, they were just old people who wanted their
peace. Why couldn't they understand that? And she added
that they could easily be her sons—or her grandsons.*

*I don't know why but somehow that seemed to calm
them down. They went off and hammered on the next door.
Tilly and me could still hear them for ages before the noise
stopped and it was finally quiet again. But it must've been
another fifteen minutes before the door was opened and we
could get out of the cupboard. Now we finally had a chance
to thank the old couple. We wanted to go then, but they
wouldn't let us. It's much too dangerous, they said, and
anyway, Tilly could hardly walk. They wouldn't let us go
just like that, they'd rather we stayed there.*

*So we went into the kitchen and they sat at the kitchen
table with us. The woman looked after Tilly's ankle, which
was blue and fat like a plum by then, and then they looked
more closely at us.*

*"Children, you're so thin!" she said even though we're
not really that thin—"and so scruffy!" Then she stood up
and laid the table. She brought out some really good stuff
for us. Probably the best they had. Saved up for Easter or
something. We didn't want to eat it at first, too embarrassed, but the two of them wouldn't let up. So in the end
we started digging in.*

*"So now, tell us," the man said when we were finished.
"Where did they catch you with the paint?"*

At first I didn't know how he knew but then he pointed at my trousers. They were covered in paint! Probably from when I chucked the bucket away in the underpass. So we told them everything: what we'd been doing and why they'd been chasing us.

"Children, children, what are you doing?" the man said. "You don't know what you're getting into. You're much too young for that!"

"Young maybe, but not too young," I said. "It's not just a whim. We planned it out."

The woman shook her head and turned to Tilly. "But why must you join in, lass? Imagine if those people caught you. Doesn't bear thinking about what they might do to you!"

"Nothing worse than the boys," Tilly said. "Doesn't make a difference. Why should I stay at home just cos I'm a girl?"

They looked at each other and seemed pretty unhappy. You could tell they were really worried about us. They lectured us for ages, but in the end they realized they wouldn't change our minds.

"It's not that you're wrong in what you're doing," the man said. "But it won't make any difference. No one can do anything against the Nazis, least of all ordinary people like us. You'd need someone up top to get rid of them."

"But who?" I asked. "The ones who could've are gone. All banged up or bumped off. No one's left!"

"Yes," Tilly said. "And anyway, who says you can't do anything? Maybe we just need enough people to work together. Whether we're ordinary people or not. We just need enough of us!"

The man shrugged. "But there'll never be enough. And don't go thinking hunger or air raids'll change that. Quite the reverse! They just make people think only of themselves. It's always been like that, and it always will be."

It sounded pretty depressing the way he said that, and we didn't answer. The woman cleared the table and it was quiet for a while.

"Maybe you don't know," the man said. "But there's a lot of talk round here about the things written on the walls."

Me and Tilly looked at each other. That was the first we'd heard of it, no one had ever said anything to us about it.

"What do people say?" Tilly asked.

"Depends who you talk to. Some would love you to be caught or at least for you to stop of your own accord. They're afraid it'll make trouble for everyone. But you're saying what lots of people feel. They'd sign up to your slogans if they dared. But…" He leant forward and looked at us, "don't be fooled. If it gets serious, nobody here will help you."

"Nobody?" Tilly said. "So why did you help us?"

"Oh, lass, we're old," the woman said. "We haven't long left either way. So not much scares us. But you're young, you've got everything ahead of you. You mustn't throw your lives away!"

We sat with them a while longer, then we stood up and wanted to go. But they held us back again. They thought there might be patrols out, waiting for us. And anyway, Tilly still couldn't walk properly. So it'd be better for us to stay—till morning, when the coast was clear.

We talked it over and saw that they were right. There was an old sofa in the kitchen. The woman made it up for us and we spent the night there. Under a cuckoo clock with a bird that stuck its head out and squawked every quarter of an hour.

I'll never forget that night. And definitely not what the old couple did for us. It's good to know that there are still people like that. But all the same: what the man said is sort of sad. It kept going through my head today. And I thought, who knows? That old boy's seen a lot in his life. Maybe he's right. Maybe it really is useless, what we're doing.

1st April 1944

Things are slowly getting serious. Me and Tom are seventeen now and a few weeks back we found our call-up papers for the military training camp in the letter box. We'd really hoped to get out of that cos we're not in the HJ but we were wrong there. They're nabbing all the apprentices who were born in '27, one firm at a time, and now's the turn for Ostermann and Klöckner and a few others.

166

Tom and me put our heads together and talked about whether to duck it. But there was no point. Work made it clear what would happen if we didn't go: we could stick any indispensable war-work status where the sun doesn't shine and be freed up for the army on the day we turned eighteen.

Fine, we thought, Plan B then. We'll go along but get on people's nerves so much that they send us home after three days tops. It was meant to last three weeks and we really didn't feel like being away from Tilly and Floss that long, or not seeing the others either.

So we set off three weeks ago on Sunday to Burg Vogelsang in the Eifel. Castle Birdsong: sounds like paradise, but right from day one we saw it was actually hell. The trainers weren't from the HJ or anything like that, but the worst slave drivers from the army and the SS. Pretty much the toughest nuts I've ever seen.

We'd barely arrived when we were sent out into the grounds. Always on the double, with kitbags that weighed a ton. And every time we reached a mud hole, one of the trainers would yell, "Air raid! Take cover!" So we'd be in the puddle, and they were all still icy from the winter, it was freezing cold. The moment we were in, it'd be, "False alarm! Get up at once!" And then they'd knock us about every which way cos we'd made our kit dirty. So back to barracks at the double and get everything clean in under ten minutes. Anyone who didn't manage it got sent back out and the whole game started again.

And that was just the first day. It slowly built up from there. Drill, marching, cross-country runs, assault courses, shooting from morning to night, and then more marching just for a change. And pack drill to punish the smallest mistake till you were ready to drop, with Tom and me always in the spotlight cos, unlike the HJ, we're not used to keeping our gobs shut when someone messes with us—trainer or not. I don't think there was one evening we could see straight the whole time.

And what's it all for? So the army don't have to spend ages training their new soldiers and can pack them straight off to croak at the front. That's the only point of the thing when you think about it. I'm ashamed of playing along. But what choice did we have?

Today we came home, the three weeks are up. All my bones are aching and Tom's the same. But we learnt some things for life: the quickest and neatest way to shoot, stab or choke other people, how to shred them with hand grenades and loads of other ways of slaughtering them. There are no flies on us in that respect now. So that's something!

2nd April 1944

Today we finally met the others again after three weeks of darkness and shame. It's Sunday, the winter's over, we got out of the city and really stretched our legs. Me and Tom told them what the camp was like and the others made fun of us. Every time we passed a puddle, Ferret yelled, "Air raid! Take cover!" until we were sick of it and ducked him in one.

"Hey, we'll have to watch out for you two," Flint said, while Ferret shook the water out of his clothes. "You're total fighting machines these days. Absolute killers! We wouldn't know you."

"If it's killers you want, pop over to Burg Vogelsang and have a look at the trainers," Tom answered. "We're still us, no fear. It'd take more than three weeks to turn us."

We stopped for a rest in a field somewhere at lunchtime. The others told us what's been up in Ehrenfeld in the last few weeks and then we got talking about our plans for this year.

"There's one thing for sure," Flint said. "All this boot-licking at work, just to stay exempt, is really starting to get on my nerves. Been talking to Knuckles. Reckon we'll get out of here and go underground soon. We've been thinking about where to go. But we're not quite ready to talk about it yet."

Lanky asked if there's room for him wherever they want to hide. He'll be eighteen soon too and has a bad feeling that they've got him on a blacklist in his factory and will offer him up to the army.

"Sure," Flint said. "The place we've got an eye on isn't meant for giants like you but we'll squeeze you in somehow. Same goes for all of you. Whatever happens and wherever

me and Knuckles land up, the Ehrenfeld EP stay together.
You can count on that!"

"Sometimes I imagine getting away from here," Maja
said. "Just right away from here, you know."

"Yes, to the Felsensee maybe," Ferret suggested. "We
could live in one of the caves and eat the bats. Till the war's
over!"

"I don't mean the Felsensee. I mean right out of this
crappy country!"

"Well, I know where me and Knuckles would go," Flint
said, putting his arm round Knuckles's shoulder. "We'd go
to sea as sailors, wouldn't we, old lummox? Imagine, Cape
Horn, Shanghai, Frisco, Rio de Janeiro! We'd have a girl
waiting for us in every port. They'd be mad for us cos we're
such fine fellows, and they'd be longing to marry us on the
spot. But not us, man! At the crack of dawn, we'd creep
out of their warm nests, back to the ship—and we'd be off
again on the high seas. Ah! That's the life, people!"

"Me and Tilly, we'd go to Australia," I said.

"Why Australia?"

"Yeah, why Australia?" Tilly asked. "That's the first
I've heard of it."

"You don't need to hear about it—I'd just pack you
in my suitcase and take you with me. And it's obvious why
Australia: there's no war there. I mean, it's everywhere
now. Even on the sea. But not in Australia. And there
aren't so many people there either. So they can't all get on
your nerves."

Floss looked at Tom. "What about us?"

"We'll go to Canada," Tom said. "We'll live in a cabin in the woods and be trappers."

"Yes, and we'll have dogs and cats and a whole heap of kids," Floss said.

"Obviously. And the only people we'll have contact with will be an old, forgotten tribe of Indians nearby. And you all, of course. Cos you'll come by and visit us now and then."

"I'll be a minstrel and travel the world," Goethe said. "Once around the globe. And then I'll start again from the beginning. And wherever I arrive for the second time, the people will still know my songs from the first time because they heard them as children." He looked at Maja. "I'll take you with me. You'll have to accompany me on the guitar."

We sat there for ages, spinning yarns. People kept coming up with better ideas of where to go and what to do. We all had our own dreams. The only thing we agree on is this: none of us will take part in this damn war—never.

Whatever it costs.

On one of the first days of the new year, I went to the home to visit old Mr Gerlach as usual. The porter knew me by then and normally let me in without a word, but that day was different. He called me over.

"You can't go and see Mr Gerlach today," he said.

"Why not?"

"He went into hospital three days ago. On New Year's Day."

"Hospital! It's not serious, is it?"

"You'd better ask him that yourself. I don't want to tell you the wrong thing."

I found out which hospital he was in, and headed over there. On the way, a thousand thoughts were chasing through my head. Of course, I'd noticed that his health wasn't the best. On my last visit, a coughing fit had brought up blood. But I had no idea how bad it really was.

When I got to his room, he was lying in bed, staring at the ceiling. There were two other men in the room, which had three beds. He was hooked up to all kinds of tubes, almost like a puppet on its strings. I gulped when I saw him. Only the fact that his bed was right by the window made things look a little more friendly.

When he spotted me, he looked pleased, yet embarrassed that I was seeing him in that condition. I sat on the bed and asked how he was.

"Ah, so over the top to stick me here in hospital," he batted the question away. "Doctors always make a fuss. I could just as well have stayed at home. I'd be no sicker there than here."

"But—what kind of illness is it?"

"Oh, it's just the cold, it's the same every winter. Especially January, that's when it's worst. It gets into my bones and my lungs, you know. No need to worry. In the spring, everything looks different, you won't recognize me."

He said it so lightly that my fears vanished at a stroke. From then on, we never mentioned his illness. We talked about his diary and all the things that were connected to it, and soon it was as though we were back in his flat and all the tubes and strange equipment around him didn't really exist.

I'd already stood up to leave when he asked, "Will you do me a favour?"

"Of course. Whatever you want."

"Please look after my birds. They need feeding and fresh water. And you have to let them fly now and then, so they don't seize up. Will you do that for me?"

I promised and said goodbye. I spent the next few days alternately visiting him and his birds. The visits became so normal that I didn't even think about it any more. There was an astonishing intimacy between us.

A few days later, when I was with him at the hospital again, something strange happened. It started when a nurse fetched him for a check-up. It wasn't meant to last longer than fifteen minutes, so I decided to stay and wait for him to come back. Just after he'd gone, the phone beside his bed suddenly rang. At first I didn't take any notice, but then it occurred to me that it might be important, so I picked it up and answered.

At the other end of the line, I could hear someone breathing, but nobody spoke.

"Hello!" I repeated. "Who's there?"

The breathing stopped. It was quiet for a few seconds, then there was a strange sound, like a suppressed sigh, down the receiver. It was immediately followed by the dialling tone. Whoever had called, they'd hung up.

I shrugged and walked over to the window. The breathing was still sounding in my ears. And then suddenly I remembered the figure. The person who'd been standing in the garden at the home.

21st July 1944

Over the last few weeks we've kept getting our hopes up,
then being disappointed. First we had to do without our
Whitsun trip to the Felsensee, which was damn hard.
But there's practically no transport running properly.
And besides, we couldn't risk running into the arms of a
patrol. Specially not now that Flint, Knuckles and Lanky
have chucked in their jobs and gone underground. For
them, getting caught would be fatal—and that's not just
words.

But then after Whitsun, something happened that
cheered us up again: the Allies landed in Normandy. The
Nazis tried to play it down—said they'd repelled the inva-
sion. But then the truth came out. Bit by bit, the Allies dug
themselves in along the coast and every bulletin raised our
hopes. France isn't far away, we thought. Maybe this whole
ordeal will be over soon, and we'll have got through it.

Yesterday, it really did look like that for a few hours.
There was news that there'd been an attempt to kill Hitler,
and then suddenly people were saying he was dead. But
nobody knew any details. Everyone was saying something
different and you had to be bloody careful who you were
talking to. All afternoon, we hoped it was true. But in the
evening there was the disappointment. Hitler had survived,

the assassination failed. Today we learnt more. They say it was army officers. The first of them were shot overnight.

Hitler announced on the radio that there will now be a reckoning like the world has never seen. All the newspapers are foaming at the mouths. The would-be assassins are "Traitors to the People" and they're telling the German youth and workers in the factories that if anyone tries anything like that again, they should "beat them to death with their hoes and shovels, and trample them under their feet".

We'll have to be damn careful for the next little while, Lanky said when we met today and talked about it. The plot was like stirring up a hornet's nest. The perfect excuse for the Nazis to do away with anyone who annoys them. You can guarantee the spies are already out, pricking up their ears. So we all need to be cautious and not say a single wrong word. We mustn't trust anyone. Preferably not even ourselves.

5th August 1944

For the first few days after the failed assassination, we were pretty down. But not for long. Then we said to ourselves that there was no actual reason to hang our heads. Fine, it went wrong, but a failed attempt is better than nothing. Flint said that and he was quite right. Cos it shows there are still a few brave people left. Even among the high-ups.

Maybe there are more of them than we think. Maybe that was just the start!

And besides, the Allies broke through in Normandy a few days ago. Until then they'd only got a few toeholds on the coast, but now they're advancing and the army don't seem to have much to throw at them. If everything goes to plan, they said on the British radio, they'll be in Paris in a week or two.

That encouraged us. We can see our chance, and we think other people must be feeling the same. Every kilometre the Allies come closer must wake people up. They must realize that it's time to do something rather than just putting up with everything. And that this is the opportunity!

So we started our campaigns again. Me and Tilly had told the others what the old couple told us. That the words on the walls aren't pointless. That people are talking a lot about them round here. So we decided to carry on—in the hope that it'll eventually have more effect than just talk.

We went out again last night and nearly copped it. There were five of us: Flint, Knuckles, Lanky, Tom and me. It was after midnight when we started. We trudged round half of Ehrenfeld and painted our slogans on the walls. Wherever it seemed right. In the underpasses and yard entrances and later—when we realized everything was staying quiet—on the streets too.

Eventually, the first strip of light appeared in the sky. Tom and me, we wanted to stop, and not push our luck. But Flint didn't agree. Him and Knuckles had been drinking—some cheap booze they'd got left over from their dealings—and now they were dead set on going one better.

"We have to go into the lion's den," Flint said. "Direct to the HJ. Then everyone'll see there's no need to be scared of the Nazis any more!"

Tom and me were against it, we thought it was too risky, and even Lanky had doubts. But Flint was dead fired up. His eyes flickered, he was so in love with his idea. He reckoned, if we were chicken, he'd just go it alone with Knuckles. So in the end we went too. After all, we didn't want to look like scaredy cats.

When we got to the Ehrenfeld HJ hall, it was all quiet. The windows were dark and there was nobody about in the streets. It was starting to get light so we didn't hang around, just got cracking. We painted our first slogan right next to the entrance so everyone who passed would be certain to read it.

At first everything was going well. But then—just as we were nearly finished—a troop of HJ lads suddenly appeared at one end of the street. We grabbed our stuff and were set to scarper the other way, but then more came from that way too. I don't think anyone had raised the alarm, cos they were dead surprised to see us. Probably pure coincidence that they had to report for duty at that time—but it was a damn dangerous coincidence for us.

There was no way out by road. We tried to get into the hall cos we thought we could escape by the back windows. But that was a no go—the door was far too solid. We were

178

trapped. The HJers came closer and it was only when they saw what we'd done that they realized what kind of people we were. Two ran right off to fetch the police and the others—about twenty of them at least—penned us in so we couldn't move.

We had our backs to the wall and were desperately wondering what to do. One thing was clear, we had to get out of there before the police came or we were finished. But how?

The HJers came closer and closer. I could barely think, I was so bewildered. Then Flint, who was standing next to me, made a sudden move. I looked over: he'd got his sheath knife in his hand. We've all got one, even the HJers. It's good form to have one. But there's kind of an unwritten law that while you carry your knife, you never use it in a fight. We've kept to that in all our punch-ups with the HJ, however hard fought they were—and so have they. Flint was the first to break it.

Before we'd realized what was happening, he leapt forward and stabbed at one of the HJers. He twisted aside, but Flint had rammed the knife deep into his shoulder, then immediately pulled it out and jumped back again. The guy stared at him for a moment, then fell to the ground. He was pressing his hand to his shoulder, but the wound was too deep, he couldn't stop the bleeding.

For a second, everyone seemed frozen. Then Knuckles and Lanky pulled their knives too, and Tom and me copied them. We advanced on the HJers. They were probably so shocked they didn't even think about how many they were and how much they outnumbered us. At any rate, they backed away.

We left our brushes and buckets of paint behind and just got ourselves out of there. Luckily nobody followed us and we didn't meet the police either. We ran till we couldn't go any further, then we hid in the ruins of a bombed-out house. Nobody said anything, everyone knew how close it had been. We stared at the knife in Flint's hand. We'd got away with it again, but by the skin of our teeth.

13th August 1944

Our latest exploits came to the communists' attention. There are still a few of them, underground. They got in touch with Lanky. Dunno how, exactly. Maybe they knew his dad, somehow heard about us, and now they want to know who we are and what our plans are.

Yesterday, Lanky and Flint went to meet them in some secret place, to talk about whether we can help each other. At the Volksgarten today, they told us what came out of it.

"They reckoned we needn't bother with the leaflets and the slogans on the walls," Lanky said. "Wouldn't impress anyone, they said. A waste of time."

"Aha! And if they're so clever, did they tell you what we ought to do instead?" Tom asked.

"Yes, they suggested going back to the HJ and 'undermining' them as they called it. Apparently loads of them are unhappy. If we were clever about it, we could achieve a lot."

Ferret roared with laughter. "That must be the joke of the century! Folks, we're sitting here cos we want nothing to do with the HJ. Only a complete idiot would suggest something like that!"

"They're not idiots," Floss said. "They know what they're talking about. What do you think, Flint? You were there too."

"Oh, I dunno. I get a bad feeling about those types," Flint said. "I reckon they just want to use us. Get us to do their dirty work at the HJ. But when we've done it and they don't need us any more, they'll just kick us into the gutter." He looked at Lanky and shrugged his shoulders. "Sorry, man. I already told you that's how I see it."

"Yeah, but it's not fair to talk about them like that, Flint. They're risking their lives against the Nazis."

"Yeah, and I respect that. But it doesn't automatically mean they're on our side." Flint shook his head. "Wake up, people! In the end, there's nobody on our side. Not even the Yanks. What d'you reckon'll happen when they come and send the Nazis packing? D'you reckon they'll thank us for what we've done? Forget it! They'll just see us as troublemakers."

"Hell, Flint!" Tilly said. "Don't you believe in anything?"

"Sure. I believe in me. And Knuckles. And all you lot. But that's where it stops. Anyone who believes in anything else is an idiot, if you ask me."

We didn't all see things as darkly as Flint, but none of us could get on with the idea of "undermining" the HJ. Not even Floss or Lanky, although they tried hardest to defend the communists. Somehow we had the feeling that they just wanted to boss us about and push us around. And we've had enough of that for this life.

We want our freedom and that's it. And anyone who won't let us have it can go to hell.

27th August 1944

The last few days were the worst I've ever known. An endless torment of pain and humiliation and the most disgusting things you can imagine. A long nightmare and I don't know if I've survived it, or even if surviving it was a good idea.

It started last Sunday. We'd arranged to meet at the bunker cos we wanted to talk about where we go next. Lanky said he'd spoken to the communists again to tell them we don't think much of their idea and would rather keep doing our own thing. He said they were disappointed but not angry with us. They said maybe we'd change our minds and if so, to let them know.

At some point we noticed that Maja wasn't there.

That was unusual. She might not say much and doesn't always join in with things but she always comes to our meetings. I can't remember her ever missing one, normally you can set your watch by her.

But that Sunday she wasn't there. Instead, suddenly, the SS turned up. They crept up on us from all sides like they knew that they'd find us there at exactly that time. Then they collared us. We tried to fight but then they punched us in the face—except Tilly and Floss—they held back from hitting them. Then they handcuffed us and led us away. Right through the city, to Appellhofplatz. To the EL-DE House.

We soon realized that we weren't going to get away as lightly as after last year's Whitsun trip. The SS men practically clubbed us in there and pushed us along the corridor to the stairs down to the cellar. Then they pushed us down, one after the other. Didn't care if we broke every bone in our bodies.

I remember whacking my head pretty hard on the wall a few times. When I got to the bottom, I was pretty dazed. Someone grabbed me and pulled me up. It was dark, I couldn't see much, just that the bloke dragged me down a narrow corridor with doors on both sides. He opened one, pushed me through and bolted it from the outside again.

I fell on my knees and it was quite a while till I was halfway myself again. The first thing I noticed was the stink. There was a biting smell of piss and rot and it made me gag. Then I saw that I'd landed in a tiny cell, maybe

183

two metres by four, no bigger. It had a barred window up in one corner and despite it being so small, there were at least a dozen men in there, all leaning against the walls.

Two of them came over and helped me up. Before I could say anything, the door opened again and the next person was shoved in. It was Tom. I caught him. Luckily the two men held us up or we'd have been on the floor again.

"Gerlo!" Tom said when he recognized me. "Shit, man! What'll they do to us?"

"Wish I knew. Where are the others?"

"Somewhere down here. Lost sight of 'em. Maybe they're in another cell."

I listened to see if I could hear anything, then called quietly, "Flint?"

All quiet. So I tried again, louder this time, "FLINT!"

Then there was an answer. Seemed to be from the cell next door. "Gerlo? Is that you? We're here, man, Knuckles and me. Are you OK?"

"Just about. Tom's here, we—"

But before I could say anything else, the door flew open and the bloke who'd dragged us here came in. He looked round, then went at random to the first guy by the wall and rammed his fist into his face with all his strength. The man collapsed instantly. Then the bully vanished again. We could hear him shut our door and open the next cell—the one where Flint and Knuckles were. Then the exact same thing happened.

"Bloody idiot!" one of the men who'd helped us hissed in my ear. "Keep your trap shut!"

Then he pulled Tom and me to the window and looked at us. "Pigs!" he murmured. "Rounding up kids now."

"What do they want with us?" Tom asked.

"What do I know, lad? Wait and see."

"What about you? Why did they nab you?"

The man shrugged. "Cos someone told lies about me, I guess. I ain't done nothing wrong."

"How long have you been here then?"

"Ages. Four weeks or so."

"Four weeks? Bloody hell!" Tom pointed to the others. "Them too?"

The man made a defensive gesture. "You're asking too many questions, lads. We don't like that down here. Remember this one thing: everyone here is innocent. Got it?"

The way he emphasized it and looked at us wasn't hard to understand. Seems there's spies slipped into the cells and he wanted to warn us not to trust anyone and not to say anything about ourselves. So we kept our mouths shut and went quiet.

We all stood there in silence for a while. Then we heard the warder—we learnt later that everyone just called him "Woodlouse"—coming down the corridor. He beat his stick against every cell door, with a steady rhythm. The men went pale at the sound, everyone stared at the floor.

The door to our cell flew open, the warder stood there. "Gescher!" he roared.

A couple of the men sighed with relief but they carried on staring at the floor. Tom winced and looked at the man who'd spoken to us.

"Go with him, lad," he whispered. "Or you'll make it worse for the rest of us."

Tom staggered out. The warder met him and the door was slammed shut again.

"What'll they do to him?" I asked the man.

"Questioning. And now shut your mouth."

I walked to the door and listened for any sound. At first there was nothing but murmuring and occasional loud voices. After a while there were some sudden dull thuds and then Tom started screaming. He screamed like an animal, and didn't stop. At one point I couldn't bear it any more and I started yelling and hammering on the door. But at once the men came and pulled me away.

The man I'd talked to held my mouth shut. "Don't upset yourself, boy!" he whispered. "You can't do nothing for your friend, he's gotta look after himself. Down here it's always best to do nothing—cos anything you do just makes it worse. So you gonna shut it, or have I got to lamp you?"

It wasn't till I nodded that he took his hand away. I could still hear Tom's screams. I faced the wall and held my ears, it hurt me so much. Eventually it was over. But then the footsteps were back and the thumping stick on the walls and the cells. Our door opened again, the warder pushed Tom in to us.

"Gerlach!" he yelled.

I just had time to see a couple of the men looking after Tom who was lying on the floor, then I had to go. My knees were like jelly. We went up the stairs and round a few corners till we stopped at a door. Behind it was the interrogation room—or the "torture chamber", as the men in the cells called it.

Inside, two Gestapo men were waiting for me—but not the ones I knew from last year. One was sitting behind a desk with heaps of papers on it. The other was standing in the corner. He wasn't in uniform, just a sweaty, dirty vest, and at first glance he looked almost like a joke. But there was something dangerous about him. Threatening. His name was Hoegen, the men downstairs told me later—and it was clear that they were more afraid of him than anyone else.

The one at the desk stared at me in silence for a while. Then he asked, "Why are you here, Gerlach?"

I didn't know what to answer. So I just shrugged. But the next moment, Hoegen was there and he gave me such a whack on the back that I tumbled forwards and fell on my knees. Then he pulled me up again.

"Try again," the one at the desk said. "Why are you here?"

"But I don't know!"

The same again. This time the clout was so hard it took my breath away. I crashed to the floor and saw stars, but Hoegen didn't give me time to get my breath. He immediately pulled me up again and the whole game started over.

They must have done it half a dozen times and every time the blows were harder and meaner. In the end, they left me lying on the floor and the one at the desk said, "Doesn't matter anyway. The question's irrelevant really. We know why you're here!"

They laughed themselves silly over that. Then they watched as I struggled back to my feet, making mocking remarks the whole time about what a fool I was, and such a wimp—they'd have to watch out in case I snapped in half on them!

When I was standing again, the one at the desk stopped laughing just like that. Then he said, "Do you know a Hilde Majakowski?"

All at once I understood. That was Maja's name! I desperately tried to work out what the question might mean. But before I could say anything, he went on, "Of course you know her, she's one of you. But there's something you don't know about her. Which is that she's working for us. So we know about everything you've done. About the leaflets, the slogans on the walls, where you meet, everything."

It was like he'd hit me between the eyes. Maja, spying for the Gestapo? Impossible! After everything we'd been through! Besides, then they could've arrested us much earlier. And they wouldn't need to question us, they could just pin us up against the wall!

"I'm sure you're wondering why we're still bothering to question you," the guy at the desk went on. "Simple, there are a few things we don't yet know. Such as who your *backers are. Or who prints your leaflets. So have you got anything to say about that?"*

I was still totally confused and even if I'd wanted to say anything, I wouldn't have been able to. He waited a moment and then shrugged his shoulders.

"Pity. But we've got time. Plenty of time. You'll tell us everything, you can count on that."

He stood up and nodded to Hoegen. Then he turned away, went over to the window and looked out. Hoegen came over.

"Trousers down!"

"What?"

He grabbed me by the neck and pushed my head down. I could smell his stinking, sweaty vest and was almost sick.

"Trousers down, you arsehole, and quick about it!"

I had to do what he said, and lean my upper body on a table by the wall. He had a kind of dog whip and then he started laying into me. At first I tried not to scream but by only the third blow, there was no chance of that. It was such hellish pain that I screamed and yelled like I'd been skewered. He wasn't bothered. He carried on, must have hit me fifty times.

When it was over, they left me lying there with my trousers pulled down for a few minutes longer, made fun of me some more and smoked a cigarette. Then they called the warder to take me down. They'd fetch me every day from then on, they said. And maybe in the night too, if they wanted me. I could look forward to it.

*Down in the cell, I crouched in a corner and blubbed.
Not even cos of the pain but because I'd never felt so
humiliated. The men looked away. Except the one we'd
already talked to.*

*"Let it out, lad, it's all free," he said. "And imagine
what you'll do to the bloke when you meet him on his own in
the park some night. That helps."*

*At some point I was over it. I talked quietly to Tom.
They'd served him up the same story about Maja but we
agreed it was nonsense. You can't be that wrong about a
person, we thought.*

*"Now I come to think about it, I haven't seen her
recently," Tom said.*

"True. Now you mention it. Nor have I."

*"What if—I mean—imagine if they'd got her before
us?"*

"You mean, the Gestapo? Here?"

*The thought was a real shock. But possible. We went
into a corner with the man who'd looked after us and
described Maja to him. With her cleft lip and all that.
Then we asked if he could remember seeing her.*

And he actually said, "Yes, I can."

"What, you saw her? When?"

*"Coupla days back. You don't see nothing of the women
here cos they've got their own cells. But once, when they were
taking me off for questioning, a girl like you described was
coming down the stairs. Must've been in before me. Won't
forget that sight in a hurry. When I got into the torture*

chamber, there was a woman with hot water, cleaning up the blood…" He looked at us and wouldn't go on. "Sorry, but that's how it was," was all he said.

We had a lump in our throats. "What do you mean, that's how it was?" Tom asked.

"Oh, stop, lads. Leave me alone. You'll only torment yourselves."

We sat there awhile, totally stunned.

Then Tom said, "So that means—she didn't tell them anything by choice?"

"Her, *by choice*? No way! Did they try that one on you?"

"Yes."

He thought for a moment and looked at the other men, then he pulled us deeper into the corner.

"Listen up now, lads," he whispered. "And don't forget this cos I ain't telling you again. The Gestapo will try anything to get stuff out of you. They'll beat your face to a pulp. Then they say your friends have talked and they already know everything. Next they promise to let you go if you tell 'em something. Come up with a new dirty trick every day. But whatever it is, you must never—never, d'you hear?—admit anything. Cos if you do, you're as good as dead. Keeping your pretty gobs shut and playing dumb is your only chance of getting out of here alive."

We made a note of it. And something else too: this bloke knew his stuff. He definitely wasn't as "innocent" as he claimed.

"Do you know what happened to Maja?" Tom asked him.

"No. I don't think she's still here." He shrugged. "Sorry, lads. But whatever they did to her, don't count on seeing her again."

He didn't want to say anything else. We crouched there together and talked about Maja. Where she could be now. And what she might have told the Gestapo. Seemed she'd at least told them where we'd meet today cos the SS knew that.

"Probably more," Tom said. "But nothing they can prove. Or they'd be acting different."

"Yes. But, Tom, I can't blame Maja."

"Me either, man! She was all alone with those brutes. Doesn't bear thinking about!"

We bunched up our fists and felt useless and helpless. Then we just sat there, waiting for what would happen. People were always being taken for questioning. Eventually that stopped and it got dark. But the cell was far too small, not everyone could lie down at once. So half of us lay on the floor and the others crouched by the walls. Every hour, when the ones crouching couldn't bear it any more, we changed, all night long. If anyone needed it, there was a bucket in the corner. Everything went in there. That was where the stink came from, and just that stopped you sleeping. It was sheer hell.

The next morning, we were knackered as anything. For breakfast, there was a beaker of water and a slice of bread *for everyone and that was it. Then the questioning started again. They got to me round lunchtime, this time I was up before Tom.*

When I went into the torture chamber, my heart almost stopped. There were Hoegen and the other one from yesterday and two boys from the HJ. I recognized them at once. They'd been with the group who caught us outside the HJ hall. The ones we'd only escaped cos Flint pulled his knife. Now they've got you, I thought. Now they'll do you over till you can't see straight!

I had to go over to them and then the desk man asked them if they recognized me and if I was one of the "graffiti bastards". They looked me right in the eye and it was clear that they recognized me just like I did them. But at first they dodged.

"I don't know," one of them said. "It was so dark."

"Dark? What do you mean, dark? What do you think this is? A children's party? You're in the HJ, you idiots, so kindly act like it!"

He looked at the other HJer. He went pale and started stammering.

"I-I-I don't think it was him."

The Gestapo guys looked like they couldn't believe their ears. They fired questions at the two of them but they insisted they didn't recognize me—whatever Hoegen threatened them with. It almost looked like they'd agreed in advance not to say anything.

Eventually, they got chucked out on their ears. "Wimps!

Bastards!" Hoegen roared after them. "You haven't heard the end of this, believe you me!"

Then he slammed the door behind them, walked to the desk and picked up his dog whip. He was seriously pissed off, bright red in the face. I had to pull down my trousers and lie on the desk. He let all his rage out on me. It was awful, just didn't stop. It was only over when I fainted.

I woke up on the floor. My whole body was one single pain, I couldn't even move. Hoegen and the warder grabbed me, pulled me out and dragged me down the stairs. In the corridor I fainted again. I don't know how I ended up back in the cell.

It was quite a long time before I was halfway with it again. Tom looked after me. I told him what had happened.

"No idea why those two covered for me. Maybe they really didn't recognize me?"

"Cobblers, they're not blind," Tom said. "Nah, believe me, they were scared."

"Scared? What of?"

"Ha, that the Gestapo would beat you to death, just on their say so. I mean, they might be in the HJ, but deep down they've got a heart. And besides, the Gestapo's over the line. Even the HJ can't stand them."

I thought nothing could be worse than the beating I'd had from Hoegen. But I was wrong. I can't even describe the stuff that happened over the next few days. Hoegen beat us with everything he could get his hands on. He knew exactly where it would hurt most and it gave him incredible pleasure. Then they started fetching us in the middle of the night when we were so confused we hardly knew where we were. They tried every trick. Put statements from the others in front of us with forged signatures to make us confess. When we didn't fall for it, they did things to us that you can't even write in a diary.

I don't know how we survived those days. Without the other men in the cell, we probably wouldn't have done. Most of them were Ostarbeiter—men from the East forced to come and work here—and they were tortured even worse than us. They told us what they do when they can't stand it any more. They think about their homes. How beautiful their country is and that they'll go back one day and see their families again. They imagine it really hard.

Tom and me tried the same thing. In the worst hours, when we thought we couldn't bear it any more, we thought about the Felsensee. About our hikes there, the comradeship with the others, messing about in the water, the stories and singing around the fire, sleeping under the open skies by the warm embers. We told each other about it and swore that we'd get there again. It was probably the only thing that kept us going.

This morning after breakfast—it was the seventh day—the warder suddenly fetched Tom and me together. We didn't go to the torture chamber but to a room on the first floor. Flint and Knuckles, Ferret and Lanky were there too. We were really shocked when we saw them, they were

*so thin and gaunt. With sunken faces, eyes deep in their
sockets—almost like ghosts. It was only when we saw their
expressions that we realized we looked the same.*

*A Gestapo man we didn't know was waiting for us.
His secretary called him "Kommissar Kütter". He laid
a paper in front of each of us, which said we'd been well
treated and hadn't wanted for anything. Sign it, he said,
and we could go. We didn't want to at first. Then he said
that in that case, sadly, they'd have to keep us there for
eternity. We looked at Flint, who nodded. So we signed.*

*"Those of you who are eighteen will report to the army
tomorrow and go straight to the front," Kütter said. "The
others are to report to the HJ and to your local police
station every Sunday morning. If there are any complaints,
you'll be back here sooner than you can blink. And now, get
out!"*

*We were more dead than alive when we left the EL-DE
House. Outside was bright sunshine and we had to hold
each other up at first, we were so dizzy after all that time in
the cellar. But we did it, we survived. And that's all that
matters.*

*I don't know why they let us out. I only know we have to
make sure we never set foot in that cursed house again. One
thing's for certain: we won't get out of there alive another
time.*

The day after I read the entry about the Edelweiss Pirates' experiences with the Gestapo, I visited the EL-DE House. I knew it had survived the war, and that it's now a memorial to the victims of Nazism. But I'd never been there, I'd never had a reason to. Now I put that right.

I wasn't prepared for what awaited me. Deep in the cellar, there was the row of cells, where the prisoners had been held, preserved as if time had stood still. I bought a ticket and went down. You could go into the cells and even the inscriptions that the desperate prisoners had scratched in the walls were still there to read. It was oppressive and felt so real that I expected to see the warder any minute, and to hear the clatter of his stick.

I crouched on the floor in one of the cells and tried to imagine what the prisoners must have felt. The fear, the pain, the hunger, the stench, the humiliation and the helplessness. Of course, I couldn't—it was beyond my imagination. But it affected me all the same; I couldn't hold back the tears from my eyes. The other visitors looked at me in surprise. But I didn't care. I could see the images from the diary before me.

The next day, I visited old Mr Gerlach and told him about it. I had to describe everything I'd observed for him, down to the last detail. He kept asking questions until he was convinced that the cells still looked the way he and his friends had found them back then. Only then did he let it be.

"Have you ever been back there?" I asked him.

"Only once," he said. "A few years ago. The area's changed a lot—only the building is the same. I stood outside it, right by the entrance. Must have spent half an hour wrestling with myself—then I left. I've never been back since."

He looked out of the window in silence. I waited a while, then I said:

"I saw the messages carved on the walls too."

He pricked up his ears. "They're still there—after all this time?"

"Yes."

"How many are there?"

"Oh, I don't know. A couple of hundred in every cell, I should think."

Some of them had stuck in my mind, and I recited them from memory. They spoke of the horrors of imprisonment and torture. But I broke off when I realized it was too much for him. There was only one more that I mentioned:

"There was one message that reminded me of you. It said: 'Rio de Janeiro, ahoy, Caballero, Edelweiss Pirates stay true'."

He sank back into his pillow. "Yes," he said and smiled, "that was one of us. It's from one of our songs."

He lay there, looking up at the ceiling. It was very quiet. It was just the two of us, the other men had turned away and were watching a programme on the televisions on the wall, with headphones on. I moved my chair closer to the bed.

"What happened to Hoegen?" I asked. "And the other Gestapo men?"

It was some time before he answered. "I don't know about most of them," he said. "But after the war, some of them were in jail for a few years, then came back to Cologne. Including Hoegen. He was a businessman I think."

"You mean—he stayed here? And people didn't chase him out of town?"

Old Mr Gerlach waved dismissively. "I saw him once," he said. His voice was dull, he'd sunk so far back into his pillow that I could barely see his face. "It was a few years after the war. When things were getting better again. I was working on a building site and after work, I liked to go to a nearby pub, for a quick beer. One evening, he was sitting there. At a table in the corner."

"Did he recognize you?"

"Oh, yes. He saw me, and then he grinned. It was a devilish grin. He knew exactly who I was."

"And you? What did you do?"

"I only had two options really," he said. "Turn around and leave right then—or kill him."

He raised his head and looked at me. Then he shrugged.
"I left."

3rd September 1944

The first thing me and Tom did after getting out of the EL-DE House and back to Ehrenfeld was go and see Tilly and Floss. Since we were arrested, we hadn't heard anything from them, and after what the man in the cell had said about Maja, we were almost sick with fear for them. We'd kept imagining what Hoegen could do to them. Those were the worst moments of all, squatting down there, knowing nothing about them and not being able to do anything for them.

So we were over the moon when we saw them again and they were both fine. They said they'd been released after two days, along with Goethe. Seems the Gestapo took them for harmless hangers-on who didn't know much. Soon as they were out, they went to our mums and told them everything and from then on, they went down to the EL-DE House every day and raised hell. About how they'd shout half the city down if they didn't get their sons back. We never heard about that, and they didn't let them down to see us either. But apparently the business got too hot for the Gestapo, and when none of us admitted anything, they had to let us go—they just had nothing on us they could prove.

It took a few days till we were halfway back to strength. Then, one evening, Ferret suddenly drummed us all up. He was really worked up and said he knew how it had all happened. Found out by total chance cos he lives on the same road as Maja.

"It was our block warden," he said. "The bastard watched her at night, coming into the building with leaflets we were going to give out the next day. She must've dropped one and the pig found it and denounced her. By the time the Gestapo arrived, the leaflets were long gone, but they still nicked Maja."

"How d'you know that?" Flint asked.

"There's a pub on our road that they haven't shut yet. Yesterday evening, I went past and happened to see the bloke sitting in a corner with his Nazi pals. I went and listened in on them cos I thought I might hear something we ought to know. He was bragging about his heroic deeds—and he told them the story."

We were filled with a cold rage. Everything we'd been through in the EL-DE House surfaced again and we thought, so it's that miserable little rat of a spy to thank for all that!

Last night we met at Ferret's block and waited for the bloke on his round. Wasn't hard—he felt safe. We waited for him in a dark gateway. Knuckles decked him and then we covered his mouth and dragged him away. Over the road and down into the cellar of a bombed-out house where no one would disturb us.

We got to work on him down there. So he'd see for once what it's like when you're done over and can't do anything about it. When you're alone and no one's there to help.

Ferret held back so the man wouldn't recognize him. But the rest of us—me and Tom, Flint, Knuckles and Lanky—worked him over till he couldn't move.

When he'd had enough, we stopped. Well, apart from Flint. He just kept going, like he was out of his mind. He gave him a kicking, then he pulled a knuckleduster out of his pocket, and walloped him with that.

I'd already noticed that he's changed since the business with the Gestapo. Hoegen must have treated him differently from Tom and me cos he recognized that Flint's something like our leader. I don't know what they did to him—he doesn't talk about it and we don't ask—but it must have been bad. When I watched him last night, it was clear that something must've broken inside him—down there in the EL-DE House.

We were afraid he'd beat the block warden to death and tried to hold him back. But he was so out of it we couldn't hold him at all. Only Knuckles managed it, by wrapping both arms round him.

"Leave 'im be, Flint," he rumbled, pulling him away. "Just leave 'im be."

It took a while till Flint came back to himself. We'd brought some rope with us and we tied the warden up with it, gagged him and tied him to a lamp post outside, and stuck a note to his forehead saying "Nazi swine".

As we scarpered, we didn't have a second thought about whether we were right to do that. Cos what does that mean, right? Probably the law's on that bastard's side. As a block warden, it's his duty to report suspicious people. Yes, he's only following the regulations. Only obeying the law. But people like us have learnt since we were kids that laws aren't made by us or for us. So why should we stick to them?

We still haven't heard from Maja—it's like she's vanished off the face of the earth. We went to her grandparents but they don't know either, they're desperate. Every day, we wonder what's happened to her and where the Gestapo might have taken her. Or did she go of her own accord? Cos she's ashamed?

After everything we went through in the EL-DE House, we'd never blame her—whatever she told them. None of us would do that. We just wish we could see her again.

5th September 1944

We didn't do what Kütter ordered us to. Like hell would Flint, Knuckles and Lanky go to sign up for the army. They immediately went back into hiding, and a good bit deeper underground than before. Down to the bedrock.

The rest of us thought for a few days, and realized we'd have to do the same as them. We've got no choice. We can't go back to the HJ—specially now they called on our year group to volunteer for the army a few weeks ago. Cos we all know what "volunteer" means for the Nazis. You can guarantee that anyone in the HJ who doesn't join up will get an earful. About how they're all mummy's boys and wimps. The conscription notices are already out. Me and Tom found them in our letter boxes too—we tore them up.

There's no going back for us. Kütter was quite clear about what would happen if we don't toe the line. They'll fetch us back to the EL-DE House. And cos they know our names, addresses and where we work, there's only one way of saving our skin. We've got to chuck in our jobs and can't show our faces at home any more. We've got to go under-ground and somehow fend for ourselves.

"Welcome to the club," Flint greeted us when we met up to discuss it. "And don't fret, if we hang in there, we'll all get through. The main thing is to find some decent lodging for us all. But I'm working on something, wait and see."

It took a few days before he showed us his "lodgings": an old, overgrown allotment with a little cottage on it, outside the city, by the railway line to Aachen. The garden belongs to a friend's parents, he said. But they were killed in a bombing raid and since then it's been abandoned.

"So, you'll see," he said, "it's pretty out of the way, but that has its advantages. You'd need a whole heap of coincidences before anyone finds you out there."

We went to look at the cabin. It's a tight squeeze for all of us together but—so what? It's a roof over our heads, and not a bad one at that. So we packed up our stuff and moved over there. We didn't tell anyone where it is, not even our mums. They're not exactly thrilled by what we're doing, least mine isn't. But I explained that it's for the

204

best, and that I'll look after her as well as I can. So she let me go.

Last night we had a housewarming: Flint and Knuckles, Ferret and Lanky, Tom and Floss, Tilly and me. Goethe wasn't there. The EL-DE House gave him a mighty knock, even though he was only there for two days. He's not used to taking a beating and finds it hard to handle. But I think in the end he'll start missing us. Eventually, he'll join us, I'm sure of that.

We've settled in now, and we have to make sure we get by. Which isn't so easy—no wages and no ration books, etc. But we've got Flint and Knuckles. They know how to get hold of stuff. They'll show us what to do.

And besides, the war's nearly over, it's as plain as the nose on my face. Maybe there's only a few more weeks to get through. Maybe this mess will all be over sooner than we think.

20th September 1944

The Allies are coming closer every day. While we were in the EL-DE House, they marched into Paris. Then it was the turn of Brussels and Antwerp, and a load of other cities we'd never heard of before. Our army can't hold them back any more. They're just putting off the end.

We wondered whether to restart our campaigns. But the memory of the EL-DE House was too fresh, we'd rather keep quiet for a while. Besides, we've got enough to do with just getting by, we don't need any more bother.

There are enough dangers as it is, as Tom and me experienced ourselves yesterday. We were out with Flint and Knuckles to organize a bit of food on the black market. Was a pretty good haul, we got butter and cheese and eggs and other stuff too. We shared it out, and Tom and me set off with our shares to take them to Klarastrasse.

We were careful, but we still walked into the arms of a police patrol. Fortunately, they didn't get the idea of searching our rucksacks, cos if they'd found the stuff, it would've been damn awkward for us. They just made us identify ourselves. That wasn't too much trouble, we had fake HJ passes on us, which we showed them.

"Why aren't you two at the Siegfried Line?" one of them asked.

"Why?" Tom said. "Should we be?"

"Now don't act stupider than you already are, you smart alecs. Thought you could skive, did you? About turn, quick march! You're coming along to the station."

They took us to the station and put us on a train, where there were already a few hundred HJers. We wanted to make ourselves scarce again, but before we could, the train began pulling out. That was when we found out what it was all about. We knew they were extending the Siegfried Line to hold the Allies up. But not that all boys our age were being conscripted for it—and all the teachers too, after the schools were shut.

We travelled about an hour and then walked a few kilometres more, and there we were. Somewhere on the flat, near Aachen. When we arrived, we couldn't believe our eyes. As far as the eye could see, there were thousands of boys, digging like moles. They had to dig out anti-tank ditches and build dugouts. Some of them were up to their knees in mud.

One of the HJers made a speech to brief us. We shouldn't get any ideas about bunking off, he said. They'd catch us, and then we'd wish we'd never been born. Then they gave out hoes and spades. So we had no choice but to join in. Not that we exactly busted a gut over it. Most of the time, Tom shovelled a bit of earth over to me and I passed it back to him, that was all. Every few minutes, some fella came along and gave us a mighty bawling out, but since the EL-DE House that kind of stuff doesn't impress us much.

At some point I noticed Tom leaning on his spade, and then he tapped me on the shoulder.

"Hey, am I seeing things, or is that old Kriechbaum over there?"

I looked round and then I spotted him too. He was standing a bit further along the trench, swinging his spade. We climbed up and went over. Then we watched him for a while. He was digging like crazy. But you could see he'd never done anything like it before. He was dead clumsy and not getting anywhere much.

Somehow, it did us good, seeing him down there. At school we were so small we never had a chance against him.

Now we were taller and stronger than him and got the feeling we could hammer him into the ground if we wanted to. Suddenly, we were really cocky.

"Hey, Kriechbaum!" Tom called down. "Remember us?"

He stopped digging and looked up at us. We could tell he recognized us, but he only shook his head contemptuously and turned away again. That really wound us up.

"What d'you reckon, Gerlo? What shall we do to him?"

"Dunno. Bury him?"

"Yeah, good idea," Tom said. "Hey, Kriechbaum, what d'ya reckon? We'll dig you in there—solve all your problems. Then you can spend eternity here holding up tanks!"

He acted like he hadn't heard, then muttered something like "scum" to himself. Then we really flipped. It had only been a joke about burying him, but now we really did it. The dirt just hailed down on him. Course there was a huge uproar. The HJ supervisors bawled us out and from then on, we had to slog like animals, but it was worth it. We'd wanted to get one over Kriechbaum at least once— after everything he'd done to us!

The pointless digging went on without a break till evening, then there was something to eat, then we had to bed down in one of the barracks there. I don't know how long they wanted to keep us there, probably days longer. Anyway, we weren't bursting to find out. We made our getaway in the middle of the night, while everyone was asleep, and by dawn we were far enough away that no one could catch us.

Then we spent the whole day trudging back. Kept following the train tracks cos we'd be less likely to come across a patrol than on the road. Late in the evening, we got back to our garden. The others were damn glad to see us—they'd been worried. Thought we'd landed up back in the EL-DE House.

No fear, we said. We were only doing our bit for the national defence effort, and helping an old friend with some gardening along the way. They don't lock you up for that!

22nd October 1944

Yesterday I found out that Horst's back in Cologne. Mum told me. I meet her now and then to slip her a few bits and bobs I pick up on the black market. I get a kind of guilty feeling cos I left her on her own. I couldn't help it, and didn't want to either, but it feels wrong all the same. So at least I make sure she gets some decent grub now and then.

We mostly meet at the Ehrenfeld cemetery, always on the same day and the same time. Klarastrasse is too dangerous for me now, I'm scared they'll lie in wait for me there. The cemetery is good and inconspicuous cos Mum goes there a lot anyway, to take care of Dad's grave. I hide myself in some bush or other first, wait for her to go past and wait a few more minutes after that. I only follow once I'm sure nobody's tailing her. Can't be too careful!

Anyway, she told me that Horst's back and wants to meet me. Suggested a spot in the Stadtgarten that used to be a kind of meeting place for us. So I set out today, right through Ehrenfeld. The whole place is a kind of desert of rubble these days. The Allies are flying over in non-stop bombing raids, sirens go off every day. And it's child's play for the bombers, the flak stations have been wiped out, and there's no proper defences any more. Everything's falling in on itself, everyone's just trying to survive one day at a time.

I didn't feel all that great about seeing Horst again. I was afraid he'd come down on me like a ton of bricks after what I did. Cos I didn't go back to the HJ even though he arranged it for me. Cos I carried on hanging round with Flint and the others. Cos I left Mum on her own. And then there was the stuff with the leaflets and the Gestapo! I wasn't sure how much he'd know, but I felt properly sick about it.

He was already waiting for me when I got to the Stadtgarten. The first thing I noticed was that he wasn't in uniform. That was odd in itself, but when I got closer, I realized that he'd changed in other ways too. He wasn't standing as upright as usual, was sort of stooped, and there was a look in his eyes I'd never seen before.

"Hey, man!" he said, when I reached him. "How's tricks?"

"Oh, could be worse. How about you? Since when have you been back in Cologne?"

He didn't answer, just looked at me. His gaze went right through me. Hell, what's wrong with him? I thought, but didn't dare ask.

"I heard what happened to you," he said after a while. "You and the others. You don't have to tell me anything about it if you don't want to. Or about what you're doing now, or where you all are. It's probably better if you don't, actually. I won't ask, either, OK?"

"Yes. Sure, Horst, that's fine. But—"

"And watch out for the Gestapo, d'you hear? They're mustering in Cologne. All the ones who escaped from France and Belgium. Want to really clear up, or so I heard."

I stood there, didn't know what to think. On one hand, I was relieved that he wasn't telling me off. But on the other hand, I'd almost have preferred it if he had done. Cos like this, things were kind of weird.

"Say, Horst, out there in the east, what's up there—I mean—what's it like there?"

"I'm not in the east any more. They transferred me to Cologne."

I wanted to know why. He said he just had a new role. Guard at a camp for Ostarbeiter, here in Ehrenfeld, on Vogelsanger Strasse. In the SS you didn't ask questions, that was just how things were. But I could tell by his voice that there was more to it. I thought maybe he'd messed up and they'd transferred him as a punishment. And then I finally dared to ask.

"Come on, Horst, tell me, what happened out there?"

He hesitated, then shook his head. "Can't talk about it."

"Damn it, Horst, I'm your brother. Tell me!"

It was a minute or two longer before he came out with it. He spoke so quietly I could hardly hear him. He'd spent the last eighteen months in Poland, he said. As a camp guard. They only told him on the journey over. At first he hadn't known what was awaiting him. But he soon realized. He took a deep breath. And then he told me everything. Everything he'd seen. And, worst of all, everything he'd done.

I was totally stunned. Just stood there and listened, without a word. At some point I had to sit down. It was like he'd whacked one of my legs out from under me. Cos, sure, no one's believed the fairy tale about the old folks' homes for ages now. Everyone knows that dreadful things happen out east. There are lots of rumours going round. That the Jews are being killed. But all the same, I wasn't prepared for what Horst said. It was appalling. And the worst of it was the thought that he—my brother—had been part of all that.

He talked and talked, until eventually he just couldn't talk any more. His voice failed and then he really broke down. Bawled his eyes out. That really finished me. All my life, I'd never seen him cry, it just didn't happen. I looked over and then I realized. Everything he'd believed in and lived for had been broken out in the east. There was nothing left for him. He couldn't go on.

"Horst, you've got to get out," I said to him, after we'd sat side by side in silence for half a lifetime. "You don't belong there."

He shook his head. "You can't just resign from the SS if you don't like it any more. That's not how it works."

"But—you could come to us. They won't find you."

"Under the same roof as Flint? Forget it! There'd be all hell to pay."

I tried again, but there was no talking to him. He just said again that I should look after myself and be careful, then he left.

I've been thinking about him all day. Or more to the point, about us. Remembered all kinds of things, about the old days and what we'd been through together. There's one thought I really can't shake off. What if I'd been the sports star out of the two of us and they'd wanted me at that school, not him? Would everything have happened exactly the other way round? Does everything really come down to such little coincidences? He's not a bad person, is he? He's my brother!

14th November 1944

A few weeks ago, we noticed for the first time that there are other people hiding in the allotment too. Mostly they're Ostarbeiter who've escaped from the camps and are now trying to scrape through till the war's over.

Lanky says there are a couple of million of them here in the Reich now. Most of them come from Poland or Russia. They were just grabbed off the street in broad daylight and carted off here, and now they have to do the most dangerous and difficult work. Without them, the war effort would have collapsed long ago.

We've made friends with the ones here in the gardens. They ran away from the camp on Vogelsanger Strasse and they've settled in a cottage near us. They were suspicious of us at first but then they warmed up. Soon as they noticed we're not Nazis, just poor sods like them.

We help each other out when we can. They don't speak good German cos they're all from Russia but they're kind-hearted people. Goethe's dead taken with them. They often sing their songs when they're feeling homesick, and he can't get enough of that. They're sad songs but really beautiful, and he plays along on his guitar. That's why he's here with us again. But we always knew he wouldn't last long without us.

The Russians told us what things were like in the camp where they were. They were herded up together in dark barracks and had to sleep in bunks that were three or four beds high. Had to slave in the factories from dawn till dusk and got hardly any food. They were so hungry they stuffed clumps of grass in their mouths. And if the guards caught them at it, they'd beat them half to death.

When I heard that, I couldn't understand how Horst can work there—after everything he experienced in the east.

And I still can't get it into my head. Tilly says they spent six years forcing their rubbish down his throat in that school, and you can't just shake stuff like that out of your clothes. She's probably right. But I'm still disappointed in him.

We remembered what happened to us in the EL-DE House. There were lots of Ostarbeiter in the cells there too. They helped us and encouraged us, even though they were even worse off than us. We haven't forgotten that and now we want to give them something back. About a week or so ago, we crept up to the camp at night and secretly slipped some stuff under the fence for them. Bread and sausage and cheese—whatever we had spare. As we were skedaddling, we could see them coming out of the darkness like ghosts to get the stuff.

We've done it a few more times since then. Least it's something we know is worth doing. Unlike the leaflets and writing on the walls. The communists were right about that: it never did any good. It was for the birds, people aren't interested. But this is different, at the camp we're really helping. Even if it's only a little thing: it's a good feeling.

When I saw Horst again yesterday, I didn't want to tell him about it. But then we got talking about the camp and in the end I did. He was appalled.

"Are you out of your minds?" he said. "Germans are forbidden from contact with the Ostarbeiter. Let alone helping them. It's a hanging offence. They'll have you right up against the wall if they catch you!"

215

The longer he talked like that, the more furious I got. *What gives* him *the right to say that stuff to* me? *After everything he's done! Eventually I flipped and yelled at him. All my disappointment flooded out. "Arsehole" I called him, and every other bad name that came to mind. He just sat there and didn't say a word. All at once he looked dead small and helpless.*

"We've been expecting them to have us up against the wall for ages," I said, when I'd blown off steam. "That's nothing new for us. We've never let that stop us, and we won't now. We've got nothing to be ashamed of, man."

Then I walked away and left him there. Only last night, I was at the camp again. It was almost like I was forced to. Like I had to prove to Horst that he couldn't boss me around any more. That I'm my own man and know for myself what to do and what not to do.

I wasn't alone. Tilly, Floss and Tom were there too. During the day, we'd traded a few cartons of cigarettes that Flint and Knuckles had pinched from somewhere for something to eat, and we had the leftovers in our rucksacks. There's a spot where the bushes come right up to the camp. We'd crept up there, and while we were at the fence, we started unpacking everything and pushing it through the wire.

Normally we're long gone when the people fetch the stuff. But last night was different. Some of them came while we were still there. They looked half starved, almost like corpses, and immediately fell on it all. We couldn't get the food through the fence as fast as they were bolting it down. It was really frightening to watch them.

When we had nothing left, they wanted to thank us. A woman stuck her hand through the fence and laid it on Floss's head, another was about to do the same to Tilly. But before she had the chance, suddenly searchlights went on, and all at once the whole fence was a blaze of light. Then there was shouting, orders being yelled somewhere, we could hear the clatter of boots.

The Ostarbeiter ran away in all directions and tried to get back into their barracks before anyone caught them. We bolted through the bushes. But we weren't fast enough. When we got out on the street side, there were already a few guards there, blocking our path. They pointed their machine pistols at us and forced us to the fence. We had to put our hands up like hardened criminals, while they hunted through our rucksacks.

It was only then that I saw that Horst was one of them, and I think he recognized me at the same moment. He twitched and stared at me, and for a moment it seemed like he didn't know what to do. Then he turned to the other guards.

"Well, all-clear then," he said. "Just a few snotty brats. Probably don't even know what they're doing is illegal. I say we just teach 'em a lesson and let 'em go."

But the others weren't having it. "They're old enough to know what they're doing," one said. "And definitely not as harmless as they look. Probably stole the food. Any rate, we can't let 'em go, Gerlach, you know that. If it gets out, we'll be for it."

He walked over and was about to lead us away. Then Horst suddenly took a few steps towards him, aimed his gun at him and the others and yelled at them to drop their weapons. They looked at him in total surprise and wouldn't do it at first. But he said it again and there was something so threatening in his voice, so determined and ready for anything, that they had no choice but to do what he said.

Horst nodded to us as he kept the SS men at bay with his machine pistol. Tilly, Floss and Tom ran away at once, but I stayed. I didn't want to leave Horst. I stood by the fence like I'd been rooted to the spot.

"Go on, beat it, big man," he said. "And farewell!"

I wanted to scream at him to come with me. But when I looked him in the eyes, I knew it was hopeless. He wouldn't come. Didn't want to go on.

Tilly and Tom were screaming their lungs out at me. They were already at the next street corner, waiting for me. I looked from them to Horst and back again, then went after them. At the corner, I turned back. Horst had just been disarmed by the other SS men, that was all I could see. Then Tom pulled me along.

Today, I spent the whole day hanging around near the camp cos I felt like I needed to do something. Didn't see any sign of Horst—obviously. They probably took him off somewhere else ages ago for a grilling. But he won't give us away, I'm sure of that. He'd never ever do that.

I'm not kidding myself. What he did was high treason and that's a capital offence too. But I don't want to think about it. Whenever I do, I remember when we met yesterday. Me screaming at him and everything I said. But I didn't mean it like that! It was just cos I was angry and disappointed. I've got *to tell him that!*

We can't let him hang. We've got to get him out of there. No matter how. We owe him that!

One day in January, one of the nurses called out to me as I was leaving old Mr Gerlach's room and almost out of the ward. I turned and saw her beckoning me to come back. She led me into the nurses' room and then shut the door.

"Sorry for calling after you like that," she said. "But I needed a quick word with you. I've noticed how often you're here, visiting Mr Gerlach."

"Yes. Why? Isn't that OK?"

"Oh no, it's fine, don't worry. Feel free to visit him as often as you like. I just wasn't quite sure—what your relationship to him is. Are you family?"

"No. We're not related."

"So, what then?"

I thought. What were we, actually? Acquaintances? No, our relationship was more special than just an acquaintanceship. Friends? Yes, that was closer to the mark. But for some reason—probably because the age difference between us was so big—I couldn't bring myself to say the word.

"I'm his—student," was all I said. "Yes, you could call it that."

She looked confused, but didn't persist. "You know—

whenever Mr Gerlach wakes up after nodding off for a few hours during the day, he wants to know whether you'd been there in the meantime," she said.

"Really? Why? I mean—why are you telling me that?"

She looked thoughtfully at me. "Because in all the time he's been here, you've been his only visitor."

I didn't want to believe her at first. I asked if it was possible that she was mistaken, but she said no. And I suddenly realized something: I'd practically never talked to old Mr Gerlach about his family or his friends or anything else from the present. In fact, I knew nothing at all about him—apart from the things that had happened seventy years ago.

"Here, sit down," said the nurse. I did, and she sat down opposite me.

"I need you to listen to this. You see, the thing is, Mr Gerlach hasn't got long to live."

"You mean—he's going to die? But that can't be right!"

"I'm afraid it is. All we can do for him is make the end a little easier—and a little more pleasant. And that's the reason I'm talking to you. I think you're the only person who still brings him a little joy. Will you promise me not to forget that?"

I was dumbstruck. I couldn't utter another word, just left the room in silence and took the lift down. When I got out into the street, I had to sit down for a while. Why hadn't he told me? He must have known what state he was in!

Then I realized that it just wasn't his style to make a big fuss. And besides, I thought, perhaps he had told me, in his own way. Perhaps he'd been telling me the whole time—I just hadn't understood.

28th November 1944

I still can't grasp what happened to Horst. Since Tom and Flint dragged me away from Hüttenstrasse and brought me back here, I haven't been able to get the images out of my head. The film keeps playing in a loop. Especially the moment when Horst looked up and searched for me. He was relying on me to come and bail him out of there—like he did for me at the camp. But I didn't bail him out. I failed.

Tilly tries to comfort me. She says I've got to stop blaming myself. I couldn't have done anything, it'd have been sheer suicide. She means well, but I know it's not true. I definitely could have done something—I just didn't dare. And then Tom and Flint wouldn't let me.

Today I sat under the trees behind the hut. I didn't feel like being inside with the others. At some point, Flint came and sat down with me. I could tell he wanted to talk about something. But he couldn't seem to speak, just ummed and ahhed.

"Damn it! What is it, man?" I said in the end. "If you've got something to say, spit it out and stop sitting around here like a lemon."

He scratched his head. "Well then, uh, I seem to remember once saying your brother was a bastard. D'you remember?"

"Yes. After he beat you up."

"He didn't actually… But—hey, never mind. Anyway, I'm sorry. In his way, he was all right, you know. If he hadn't gone to that crappy school, he could've been one of us."

I clenched my fists. "He was one of us, Flint," I said. "Damn it all, he was one of us."

Flint looked at me with his coal-like eyes. I looked back. This time it was him who couldn't hold my gaze.

"Yes," he said, staring at the ground. "You're right, Gerlo. He was one of us."

15th December 1944

Winter hit us hard a couple of weeks ago. It's icy cold, we're frozen to the bone. There's no heating in our hut and we've got our work cut out keeping ourselves vaguely warm. We've started burning the trees behind the cabin. But we've got to be careful that you can't see the smoke from the railway line. Otherwise we'd end up with the police—or worse—breathing down our necks in no time.

It's total chaos in town. Ehrenfeld is nothing but ruins. Everywhere you go, you have to fight through rubble and watch out in case you fall into a bomb crater or get hit by a falling wall. There's actually nothing left to bomb, but the air raids keep on all the same. Planes fly low more and *more often, strafing people, right out on the street. They almost got Ferret once. He was so desperate, he jumped into a pond, he told us, and that's what saved him. When he got back, he was so frozen through we had to thaw him out by the fire.*

Every time you walk into the city now it's a suicide mission. We only go if we absolutely have to, or we're driven by hunger. You might bump into SS or Gestapo troops anywhere. They're searching for illegals: escaped Ostarbeiter, deserters, plunderers—and people like us. If they catch some poor devil, they don't hang around, just make short work of him. They disappear behind the nearest wall, you hear a few shots. And that's that.

Sometimes you see people wandering around the ruins who don't even know who they are or where they're going. They've probably lost everything. They can't handle it, they've gone totally mad. You hear them giggling or telling stories about when they were young. In a real little kid's voice. If I see something like that, I make myself scarce and try to forget it.

Anyway, we've got enough to deal with for ourselves. Since the winter started, it's been harder and harder to rustle up any grub. There's hardly anything to be had anywhere in the city, even on the black market. We put our heads together and discussed what to do. Flint had a suggestion. Said he knew a couple of blokes. Professionals.

"Professionals?" Tilly asked. "What does that mean?"

"Well, burglars. Pros. They know where there's stuff to nick and how to get at it. And they wouldn't have anything against a few people helping them out, they said."

"Do you know them well?" Tom asked.

"What does 'well' mean? They're not exactly friends, I don't want that much to do with them. But I think they're pretty reliable—as far as people like that can be."

We spent a while talking about it. Nobody was exactly thrilled by the idea, specially not Tilly and Floss. But you could hear our bellies grumbling and we had to do something. So we decided to at least have a look at the guys.

The next day, Flint, Tom and me met up with them. Their names are Rupp and Korittke and they're pretty shady types. I didn't like them much, specially cos it was clear from the start that they don't take people like us seriously. Or only Flint—they accept him, but they see me and Tom as just a couple of hangers on, and they made no bones about that.

All the same, we soon agreed to try our luck with them. Cos we could tell they know what they're doing. They know exactly where there's stuff to be had and the best way of getting at it. OK then, we said to ourselves, they might be crooks, but they're our best hope.

So last night we went out with them for the first time. To the Ehrenfeld goods station. Flint and Knuckles were there, and Ferret and Lanky, Tom and me. They couldn't be doing with girls—Rupp and Korittke said that from the start, reckoned it would be asking for trouble. So Tilly and Floss stayed at the allotment. And Goethe stayed with them: the crooks didn't even want to meet him.

We could tell at once that they know their way around the station. Tonight a load of tinned meat and sausage was going out for the army, they said, that's what they'd set their sights on. We didn't care how they knew that. They probably bribe some railway worker to slip them some information now and then.

We crept over to the tracks. The train they were talking about was already there. It was shut and locked, there were transport cops everywhere, guarding it. No way of getting at it. We were disappointed at first and thought we'd have to chuck it, but Rupp and Korittke reassured us. Said there was bound to be an air raid warning tonight. That'd be our chance.

We must have spent an hour or two lying on the bank, waiting in the freezing cold. Then the sirens finally wailed like they do almost every night these days. The railway cops vanished into their shelters. The moment they'd gone, we leapt up and ran for it. Kept down low to the tracks, over to the goods train, and just as the first bombs exploded in the distance, we reached it.

It didn't even take a minute for the two crooks to pick the lock on one of the big sliding doors. We opened the van and were in. We were all carrying big rucksacks and we scooped up anything we could get our hands on in the dark. Then we were out and scarpering over the tracks. The raid was in full swing, they were targeting the station too, shells and high explosive bombs were going off everywhere. We ran like rabbits, all of us wanted to get away as fast as possible.

Luckily no one copped anything. We hid in the cellar of a bombed-out house and shared out the loot. It wasn't exactly a fair split. Rupp and Korittke kept the best for themselves, so they could flog it on, and left the rest for us. But we didn't say anything. We didn't want a row and were happy to have got out unscathed. So we took our stuff and beat it.

First we had a midnight feast in the allotment, and invited the Russians along too. It was the first time in ages we could properly fill our bellies. We put some stuff aside for our mums so that everyone would get something. But we don't go to the camp any more. It's too dangerous now.

This morning we didn't wake up with rumbling bellies for once. It was snowing outside, we fetched wood and got the fire going. Then we crouched round it and talked about last night again.

Tilly and Floss weren't exactly happy about what we'd done.

"It's much too dangerous," Floss reckoned. "If the transport cops see you, they'll gun you down. And don't go thinking those spivs will help you. If it comes down to it, they'll save their own skins. They don't give a damn about you."

"Yes," Tilly said. "And besides, I reckon that's taking from the wrong people. You know what's going on at the front. The soldiers are half starved. They need the food!"

But Flint wasn't having that. "Everyone has to look out for themselves," he said. "And if any of our boys out there haven't seen the writing on the wall and legged it, there's no helping them—they had it coming. Sorry, people, but that's how I see it."

None of the rest of us would have put it that bluntly, but we basically agree. We're not responsible for people who're still fighting for the Nazis. We can't be bothered about them. No one's ever bothered about us.

25th December 1944

It's the saddest Christmas we've ever known. Yesterday, we sat in our little cottage and tried to drum up a bit of cheer. Normally, we're not particularly sentimental, but sitting there in the cold was a bit much for us all the same. We wished we could go home to our mums—apart from Flint and Knuckles of course, who don't have theirs—but it was too dangerous. Only Goethe went out in the evening, wanted to slip home to his parents' place.

"I'll be back some time tonight," he said.

"Bring us some chocolate cake," Ferret called after him. "And roast pork. And potato salad. And frankfurter sandwiches. And—"

*"I'll bring you back a few songs," Goethe said. Then he
went.*

*When it got dark, there was an air raid warning,
and it started almost at once. The hits were pretty close.
We went out and saw that most of them were coming
down over Ehrenfeld. Christmas Eve of all nights! we
thought. Not that we're very religious. But all the same.
It seemed kind of mean to clobber people on a night like
this.*

*Goethe stayed away, so we settled down for the night.
It wasn't till he hadn't turned up again this morning
that we started to worry. Me and Tom went to see where
he'd got to. Normally, his parents' area doesn't get badly
hit cos there aren't any factories or workers there. But
last night was different—we saw that the moment we got
there.*

*We could see from miles off that something had come
down in Goethe's street. We got scared and started running. And then we saw what had happened: his parents'
house was totally destroyed. The whole building was rubble,
not a stone still in place. At first we didn't know what
to do. Then we ran around it, calling out, but nobody
answered. It was horribly quiet.*

*Eventually, people came from next door. Their house
had been damaged but was still standing. They told us
what happened. A direct hit, the house went up in flames
at once. Goethe and his parents got out in time, everyone
was trying to put the fire out. But then Goethe suddenly*

went back into the house—nobody knew why. Just after that, everything collapsed. It wasn't till today that they found him under the rubble, but that was far too late.

We were in total shock. Couldn't believe it at first, but the way they told us, there was no doubt. We crept back to the others like beaten puppies, and gave them the news. It really hit us hard, and we just sat around dumbly for ages.

"Why did he do it?" Floss said at last, with tears in her eyes. "Why did he go back in? What did he want?"

"Probably wanted to rescue something," Tom said. "Must have been to do with his music. What else would have been so important to him?"

"Do you remember what he said when he left?" Tilly asked. "'I'll bring you back a few songs.' Perhaps that's why he went back into the house. To get them."

That was a real blow. We were all sure she was right. Nothing else makes sense. But the idea that that's why he died was unbearable. Flint and Knuckles vanished outside, and then there was shouting. They were kicking something to pieces, blowing off steam.

The rest of us stayed inside, talking about Goethe. He was the best of us, everyone agreed. All his life, he never hurt a fly. And he knew more and could do more than the rest of us, but he never showed off. Not once. So for it to be him, of all people, who copped it is so unfair that we can't even make sense of it.

Eventually, Flint and Knuckles came back in. Flint's look was darker than I've ever seen, even on him. "That's

*it," he muttered. "We won't stand for that. They'll pay for
that. I swear it."*

17th January 1945

*For a few days after Goethe's death it was like we'd been
paralysed, but then we pulled ourselves together. Things
had to go on somehow or other, we couldn't just give up.
So we met Rupp and Korittke again and went back out
raiding. We got more and more daring. Over time we
started to get a real "what the hell" feeling, specially Flint
and Knuckles.*

*About a week ago, we almost came a cropper. We
were at the goods station, for the second time in a couple
of days. We waited for the sirens as usual and then crept
over to the train the two crooks had scouted out. But
when we got there, the doors suddenly burst open and a
troop of transport police who'd been lying in wait for us
burst out.*

*We immediately scattered, legged it over the tracks.
They were shooting at us, we had to keep jinking and
sidestepping so they didn't hit us. The only one who got hurt
was Lanky, but it was harmless, just a graze on his shoulder. Tilly and Floss bound up the wound when we got back
to the allotment. We really were bloody lucky.*

*The next day, Flint vanished a while, and we had no
idea what he was up to. When he got back, he drummed*

us all up. He waited till everyone was there, then pulled something out of his pocket and put it on the table. A pistol. Military issue.

At first we just sat there, staring at Flint and then the gun and then back again. It was dead quiet. Looking at it gave me a bad feeling. The others felt the same, you could tell.

"Hey, Flint!" Lanky said in the end. "What d'you want with that thing?"

"Huh, what d'you think? D'you think I'm just going to look on as we bite the dust one by one? Goethe and Gerlo's brother have already copped it, you were nearly for it yesterday, and we've never heard from Maja again, have we? I think it's time we paid them back in the same way."

Knuckles nodded, seemed to think the same. But the rest of us were less keen, specially Floss.

"I don't know, Flint," she said. "I'm afraid we'll just make everything worse. If we start doing stuff like that, they really will take notice of us!"

"We don't have to start anything," Tom said. "But that thing's good life insurance. We can take it with us when we go out at night. To defend ourselves."

"Defend?" Flint said and shook his head. "Tell me this, Tom, when they pissed on us and beat us up at the Felsensee, when they shaved our heads and beat the shit out of us in the EL-DE House—were they defending themselves?"

"No, of course not. Why?"

"Just because. Think about it, man."

A few days later, on our next mission, Flint had the gun with him for the first time. In a way, we felt safer with it. All the same, I was damn glad there were no incidents. I wasn't keen to find out how far Flint'd go.

But last night we did. We wanted to do the station over for the very last time. In fact, we'd meant to stop after the trap the railway cops had set for us—the place was too hot for us now. But Rupp and Korittke had done so well out of the stuff from the trains that they really wanted to go back again—and we got talked into going along with them.

At first, everything seemed to be going smoothly. The train wasn't even guarded, we got in with no problems. Rupp and Korittke broke open the door quickly and easily, we were about to jump in—but then we saw that the van was empty. Completely empty. At the same moment, search-lights went on and the whole train was suddenly flooded with bright light. Someone yelled at us from somewhere to come out with our hands up.

Before we knew what was happening, Flint roared at us to take cover and then he pulled the pistol and started shooting. We hurled ourselves into the gravel between the tracks. From the corner of my eye, I saw Rupp and Korittke draw their guns too and then the shoot-out started. It was ear-splitting, we just kept our heads down.

I couldn't tell who'd been lurking in wait for us. Probably the security service, maybe some SS too. Either way, Flint hit one of them in the exchange of fire. We could hear him yelling and groaning. That seemed to distract them, cos they stopped shooting for a short time. We took the chance to crawl under the train, climbed over a wall at the other end of the station and got away.

Back in the allotment we were relieved that nothing had happened to us—but pretty shocked too. Except Flint— he was on top of the world.

"Now we've finally shown them for once," he said, constantly prowling round the table. "I told you, people. Can't keep running away and hiding and being scared! Now it's our *turn*. Now we'll get our revenge for what they've done to us."

He was really whipping himself up. The rest of us just sat there, listening. Tilly and Floss crouched on their chairs and looked kind of glum, but they didn't say anything. It wasn't till later, when we'd settled down to sleep in our corner, that I asked Tilly what was wrong.

She pulled the curtain over like we always do when we want to be private. "D'you actually realize that Floss and me are shit scared every time you lot go out?" she whispered. "There's no need to make that worse, is there?"

"But we can't help it, Tilly! We've got to live on some- thing, haven't we?"

"Ah, hell, that's not what I mean at all."

"What is it then? The gun?"

She groaned quietly. "Yes, that too. But not just that. There's something else. Flint—he's been scaring me lately. He's changed. I get a bad feeling round him."

"Oh, Tilly, listen here," I said and pulled her to me. "You really are the best thing I've got, do you know that? Sometimes I even let you tell me what to do, and not many people can say that. But I won't hear anything against Flint. Without him, we'd have been six feet under ages ago. You've got to trust him. He'll get us through."

"Yes, I know. He always has so far. But did you hear him?" She whispered even more quietly. "We've got no right to shoot people! Stealing food to stay alive, yes. Defending ourselves if we're attacked, yes. But we can't go killing people!"

"Seriously?" I said. "What does that even mean? I'd be amazed if you can explain it to me. I don't know any more, anyway."

She shifted a fraction away from me. "Would you join in? I mean, could you join in?"

"Ah, I don't know. Probably not. But sometimes—if I think about Horst, or Goethe or Maja—there's such a mad fury that I don't even know who I am. No idea what I might do in moments like that."

It had got dark but I could feel that she was shocked. "You mustn't!" she said. "If you did something like that, you wouldn't be the same person to me."

"Maybe I'm not anyway, Tilly. Maybe I haven't been since the EL-DE House."

She lay there in silence for a while, then she came closer again. "One day we'll live together in peace. Got that? Just us two. In a little cottage by a lake. And we'll have kids.

They'll always have enough to eat. And they won't even know the word war."

"Oh, Tilly," I said. "Don't kid yourself. It's pointless wishing for things that'll never happen. Even if there are no more Nazis some day, it won't change anything. The big shots will still be in charge and they'll wipe their feet on people like us. That's how it's always been. Someone up at the top always calls the shots."

"What do you mean, people like us?"

"Well, people who don't care about heaping up piles of stuff. Who want nothing more than air to breathe, a path to walk down and a song to sing. They'll always push us around—wherever we end up."

I found myself thinking about that conversation a few times today. Now I'm sorry that I interrupted Tilly's daydreams. Actually, I like it when she's like that. I was just in a bad mood. I'll tell her soon. Just got to wait for the right moment.

24th January 1945

I wanted to throw this diary in the fire and burn it. Even stood there with it in my hand. I've never shown it to anyone except Tilly and now that's not possible. Everything's so pointless now.

I did keep it in the end and I'm still writing in it, but I don't know why. Perhaps I imagined that I could lock the worst things up in it and then shut them all away together. And then they'd be forgotten for as long as I want to forget them—but still not lost.

It's hard to write about it. I don't know where to start. Maybe with Lanky getting together with one of the Russian women. Her name's Nadia and she's one of the ones living here in the gardens. A few days ago, she told him that there's a clothes depot near the goods station that the Nazis and their families are still using to get the best stuff for themselves. She said she worked there with a couple of other women before she escaped.

When we heard about it, we got curious. We desperately need new winter clothes cos our old ones are torn and full of holes and don't keep the cold out any more. So we decided to get into the depot. But without Rupp and Korittke. Them two have been getting on our nerves for ages. Besides, Flint reckoned he and Knuckles had been watching and cribbed everything they needed to know off them. They'd got the right tools too. We didn't need those blokes any more: they could take a running jump.

Three days ago, we set out. It was late in the evening, late at night even. Everyone was there, even Tilly and Floss and Nadia and a couple of their friends. Nadia showed us where the warehouse is. Between a couple of overgrown train tracks that aren't used any more. We'd always thought it was an old factory building, empty for ages. None of us had any clue what was really in there.

Flint and Knuckles went ahead to scout the area out.

Nadia had told us the place isn't guarded at night, but after our recent experiences, we wanted to be on the safe side. After a while, the two of them came back to get us, said it was all clear. We went to the depot, and Flint and Knuckles tried to break one of the iron doors in with their tools. They weren't as quick as Rupp and Korittke, it took a while. But in the end they managed it and the door was open.

Ferret and one of the Ostarbeiter stayed outside as lookouts, the rest of us crept in. A couple of us had torches. When we switched them on, we couldn't believe what was there in front of us. Compared with what we and most people in Ehrenfeld are used to, it was a real wonderland. Everything you can imagine: suits, evening dresses, even fur coats, and so many of them, more than we'd ever believed possible.

"So much for national community!" Lanky said, after we'd stood there speechless for a while. "I wouldn't mind burning this place down."

"Maybe we will," Flint said. "But not yet. First we'll take what we need."

We swarmed out and walked along the shelves, everyone gathering up something that fit. Mostly we just put the new gear on right away and left our old stuff lying there in exchange. What did we want with it anyway? None of us has a wardrobe or anything.

When we were sorted, we met in the middle of the hall again. We wanted to beat it, but Tilly, Floss and Nadia couldn't get enough of the stuff. They'd found a shelf of dresses like they'd never worn in their lives and were longing to know what they looked like in them.

"We'd better get out of here!" Flint said. "There's no time for a fashion show!"

But Tom and me took the girls' side. "Why not?" Tom said. "Let them, Flint. Won't do any harm."

The three of them showed us the shelf, then they tried on some of the dresses. But they couldn't make up their minds, kept finding even more beautiful ones, and then they had to try those on too. We sat around them in a circle, shone our torches on them and whooped them on. Actually, they were thin as rakes, just like us, starving and with filthy faces. But that night it didn't bother us: we thought they were gorgeous.

It was the first time in ages that we'd forgotten everything around us and just messed around. Like the old days. At the Felsensee or when we glued the block warden to the windowsill or played cat and mouse with the cops in the park. For a few minutes, it was like that again. Even Ferret and the other guy who were meant to be lookouts came in and sat with us. We stopped believing that bad things could happen.

I don't know where the security guards suddenly sprang from. Probably a police patrol on their beat. They came in without us noticing and then just opened fire without warning, like they always do with plunderers. Floss and Nadia took cover but Tilly wasn't quick enough. One of the *bullets hit her. I don't think she felt a thing. Didn't even groan. Bullet must have got her right in the heart.*

I can just remember Flint and Knuckles pulling out their guns and shooting back. Dunno how we got out of there. Floss said Tom and Lanky pulled us out somehow—her and me. I don't remember a thing. Don't want to.

The thought of Tilly being dead and us having to leave her there is driving me half crazy. There was so much I still wanted to say to her. Now I feel paralysed. I don't know how I'm meant to go on—without her.

The last time I saw old Mr Gerlach was the day before he died. When I walked into his room, I hardly recognized him, and even if the nurse hadn't spoken to me, I'd have realized by then, at least, how sick he was. He couldn't stand any more; his face was pale and sunken. It was hard for him to breathe and when he said anything, he spoke so quietly I could hardly make out the words.

So for most of the time, I just sat quietly by his bed. From time to time he nodded off. When he opened his eyes again, he looked for me, and he seemed to grow calmer as soon as he spotted me. I spent many hours with him that day. He was alone in the room by then; the other two men had been moved somewhere else. Only a nurse came in now and then, but otherwise we were undisturbed.

When it got dark outside, it was time for me to go. I bent down to him, to say goodbye and to tell him I'd come again the next day. He looked at me and nodded, but there was something in his expression that held me back. I hesitated, then I suddenly remembered what the nurse had said: that nobody but me had visited all the time he'd been in hospital.

I pulled the chair out again and sat down. "Oh, by the way—what happened to you and Tom in the end?" I asked him. "You were such good friends—and now you never talk about him. What happened after the war?"

"Oh, he moved away," he whispered. "Down south. Floss had family there. In the country. Things weren't so bad down there."

"But you kept in touch with him?"

"We wrote. He and Floss got married and had children. Then we wrote less. Christmas and birthday cards. Eventually that stopped too. A new life—and you don't want to be reminded of the old one."

I stood up and was really about to go, but he beckoned me back once more.

"Something like I had with Tilly," he said, "only happens to you once. If you're lucky! Never happens for lots of people. And you only meet someone like Flint once too." He sank into his pillow and sighed. "And I was his friend!"

Suddenly he stretched out his hand to me. I took it and squeezed. It was the first and last time that we touched.

"You see, Daniel, I have nothing to complain about."

I wanted to say something else. But when I looked at him, he was already asleep again.

25th January 1945

I spent the last few days lying in the cottage in complete despair, just feeling sad and blaming myself in thousands of ways. Tom and Floss tried to talk to me but I didn't want to. Everything seems pointless to me—now that Tilly isn't here.

It wasn't till today that I managed to get myself together. There's still the despair but now there's a great canyon of anger too. I went to Flint who was outside the hut with Knuckles.

"Give me your pistol!" I said to him.

He gave me a totally stunned look. "Hey, Gerlo—don't you think you should…?"

"No. Stop talking and give it to me!"

I more pulled the gun out of his pocket than anything else. Then I set off. Right across Ehrenfeld, down Venloer, in broad daylight. Didn't give a monkey's if anyone saw me who shouldn't, or if anything else happened either. I wanted something to happen. To give me an excuse.

About level with the Stadtpark, two SS men came towards me. I didn't avoid them or run away from them like I normally would, but went deliberately up to them and barged between them. I jostled one of them so much that he lost his balance and fell into the wall. Then I walked on.

They shouted after me to stop and show them my papers. I turned and said my papers were none of their sodding business. As I said it, I was pushing my hand into my pocket—where the gun was. I was determined to shoot them if they made one wrong move.

But something must have held them back from giving me the usual treatment. They hesitated, then one gave the other, the one who'd stumbled into the wall, a nudge.

"Come on, leave the kid," he said. "He's not worth the effort. They'll have his head off at the front soon enough."

They laughed and walked on. I was trembling with rage and gripping the pistol, but that was it. I didn't draw it. I just stood there and watched them till they were out of sight, then I turned and walked on.

At some point, I reached Appellhofplatz, without having really intended to. Haven't been in that neck of the woods since last year when they let us out of the EL-DE House. Seeing it again sent a chill down my spine. At first I considered going in, but I didn't have the guts. I stationed myself in a yard gateway across the road and watched the building.

I kept it up at least a couple of hours. I was hoping the whole time that Hoegen or the Woodlouse or one of the other bullies would come out. I definitely hate them enough, I thought. I'd definitely pull the trigger on them. And they definitely wouldn't be missed.

But it was like I was cursed. Not a single one of them appeared. It was almost ghostly quiet on the street—like

*I was the last human in the world. Or like everyone had
agreed not to cross paths with me. When it got dark, I left.
I didn't get rid of it, of my anger.*

*Back in the allotment, I went to Flint and put the
pistol on the table for him.*

"Do you have a plan?" I asked him.

*He took the gun and pocketed it. "Knuckles and me,
we've got a few ideas. But we're still working on them."*

"Whatever it is," I said. "Count on me. I'm in."

12th February 1945

*The only thing still keeping us going is the hope that the
war will soon be over. But it's a hideous waiting game. It's
over three months since the Allies marched into Aachen.
Aachen! Back then, we thought it'd all be over by winter.
But then there was the Volkssturm—the home guard—and
anything else that came into the heads of them up top.
They've called everyone born in '28 up to the front and
people say the '29ers will be for it next. Anything on two
legs gets used as cannon fodder, just so they can put off the
end for another few months.*

*We wondered if there was anything we could do to cut
things a bit shorter. We thought of all kinds of ideas. Most
of it was so rash that we ditched it at once. In the end, it
was Lanky who had the brainwave. We're actually sitting
on the source, he said, pointing outside with his thumbs.*

At first we didn't understand what he was talking about, but then we realized he meant the railway lines. The tracks carry reinforcements for the Western Front and we'd eat our hats, we thought, if there wasn't something we could do about that.

We were like a dog with a bone with that idea—probably partly cos it gave us something to do other than just constantly thinking about all the shit things that have happened. Lanky told Nadia about it and one evening she brought one of the Ostarbeiter who are hiding in the gardens to see us. He's a railwayman, she said—or was before they dragged him here from Russia. His name was Pavel and he might be able to help us.

We told him what was floating around our heads. He was dead keen on the idea from the start, he hated the war so much. We could count on him, he said. He knew about trains. He knew how to make them derail too. Wasn't that hard. We just needed the right tools. Flint said let us deal with that. Near the goods station was a Reichsbahn repair workshop, we were sure to find what we needed there.

A couple of nights ago, we got into the repair shop and took Pavel with us. Wasn't half bad. We'd found out that there are two armed watchmen there at night. Luckily, Flint and Knuckles managed to grab them before they could raise the alarm. Knuckles sent them off to dreamland for a bit. Then we went in, rounded up the necessary stuff as fast as possible and vanished again.

We got to work the very next night. It was at the end of the goods station—where the platforms run together and the trains roll out onto the lines. Pavel explained what we had to do. We needed to put brake shoes on the rails—some of the ones we'd nicked from the workshop. They're normally used for braking the trains in the sidings. But the trick was to jam them right in the points. Then the train wouldn't be braked but thrown off the tracks.

We crept through the slush to the railway embankment and started by just lying there, watching everything. There was a full moon, we had good visibility. The trains were running on the side opposite us. Some were open and we could see their cargo: ammo, weapons, spare parts, real heavy gear. They rumbled over the points and vanished, one after another, in the dim light.

There were transport police everywhere, watching the site. It was impossible to get to the tracks without being seen. We had to wait for the air raid warning—like when we went raiding with Rupp and Korittke. They bomb the station every night these days, you can almost set your watch by it. So we knew our chance would come.

When the sirens went off, the railway cops withdrew into their shelters as usual. We waited till the first bombs came, then crept onto the tracks. They were icy and with the heavy brake shoes in our hands, we could hardly keep on our feet. But luckily we made it to the lines the trains were on without any accidents. Then we jammed the brake shoes into the points, the way Pavel had shown us.

We had to work quickly—the trains were still running through the raid—almost one a minute. From the corners of our eyes we could see that the next one was already coming towards us. It was no more than twenty or thirty metres away before we'd done it. At the last second, we jumped aside and ran away over the rails. Behind us, there was a loud screeching sound—the locomotive going off the rails. That was followed by the crash of the wagons, and shortly after that there was one sudden explosion after another. I dunno if they were bombs, or the train cargo—or both at once. Anyway, it was suddenly dazzlingly bright, all kinds of shrapnel flying around. There was a noise like the end of the world, and we just ran for our lives.

We ran away from the station and through the streets, till we couldn't go any further, then we hid in some ruins. Ferret had a lump of shrapnel in his arm. Flint pulled it out and we bound up the wound as best as we could. It was quiet, nobody said anything. We all knew that we'd been very lucky and the thing could've turned out quite different.

When the raid was over, we went back to the allotment. By then, we were over the first shock and when we told Floss and Nadia how it'd gone—the way the train blew up behind us and total chaos broke out at the station—there was only room for satisfaction. We had the feeling that we'd at least paid them back a little bit. And it felt damn good.

It didn't last long though. The business at the station was two nights ago—and today we paid for it. Or maybe *the two things aren't even linked, maybe there are just too many people hiding in the gardens now. Maybe they nabbed one or two and put them through the wringer in the EL-DE House, and they gave away the hiding place. Who knows? Don't reckon we'll ever find out.*

It was this morning, very early, it was still dark. A troop of Gestapo turned up and combed the place. Luckily, Ferret was outside already, doing his business on the railway embankment. He saw them and warned us. We crept out of the hut and hid in the bushes along the railway line. They're covered in thorns, but we squeezed in anyway. We'd rather get scratched faces than shot, we thought.

The Gestapo searched one hut after another and rounded up anything on two legs. A couple of the Ostarbeiter tried to escape, but they didn't get far. They just shot them in the back and left them lying there. They loaded the rest onto trucks and drove them away.

Lanky and Nadia were there too. Lately, they'd been sleeping at ours one night and with Nadia's people the next. Yesterday evening we were still cracking jokes when they went over to the other hut. Didn't they have a home to go to, and they should take decent, settled people like us as an example. Now we weren't in the mood for joking. We couldn't do a thing, just had to watch them being carted away.

I wonder if we'll ever see them again. And where we can go now that our hideout's been busted. When we got out of the thorn bushes, I looked Flint in the eyes. I don't think even he has an answer to that.

23rd February 1945

Horst was right when he warned me about the Gestapo. They were gathering in Cologne to really clean up one last time, he had said. And that's exactly what happened. The city's full of them. They fled from the Allies and now it's like they've got a bloodlust. Seems there's no one left to give them orders. No one to control them. They've taken control and it's a reign of terror. They're shooting people in broad daylight, or stringing them up and leaving them hanging there as a deterrent. And as for how many people are sitting in their torture chambers and dying miserably, it's best not even to think about that.

I wonder what's going on in their heads. They must know, mustn't they, that the war's lost? When there's a west wind, you can hear the front—the roar of it comes closer every day. But maybe that's just it. They know they're going under and they want to take as many others with them as possible. Thinking about it sends a chill down my spine. What on earth kind of people are they? Where does the evil inside them come from? And how did they get like that?

Since they drove us out of the allotments, we've been completely homeless. Every night we sleep somewhere else, mostly in the cellars of bombed houses. Sometimes there are still empty cupboards and chests of drawers there, which we break up and use for firewood so we've got a little heat at least. We pinch food from the depots in town. They're guarded of course, but we find a way in somehow. Usually through sewage pipes or cable ducts—we're not picky.

The stray dogs that roam the place now are dangerous. They've formed packs and they're totally feral. You have to watch out not to come across them unarmed, especially at night. We've had a few run-ins with them, when they tried to steal our food. We don't hold back when we're dealing with them. It's not like we've got anything going spare.

A couple of nights ago, Flint and Knuckles set out to break into a warehouse on the edge of town. We'd heard that there was stuff there to nick. When they came back, they really had got hold of something. Best of all, a whole crate of canned meat. It was ages since we'd had anything that good. We fell on it like wolves.

The two of them had bread, fat and sausage, too, there was enough for all of us, for several days. And then they pulled something else out of their rucksacks. Our eyes were like saucers when we saw it. Sticks of dynamite, military ones. A whole bundle.

"They looked so inviting we couldn't just leave them," Flint said. "There was more too. Reckon they want to blow the place up when the Allies come."

"What are we meant to do with that?" Ferret asked. "D'you want to blow the dogs sky high next time they rob us?"

Flint grinned. "Something like that. Only not the dogs
you're *talking about."*

We all knew at once what he meant. He waited a
moment then looked at Tom and me. "I told you, Gerlo.
And you, Tom. Someday we'll have our day of reckoning.
And how. Not the kids' stuff we've done so far."

It was quiet for a bit. Then Tom asked, "EL-DE House?"

Flint nodded. Then he explained what he was plan-
ning. We should creep up to the EL-DE House under cover
of darkness, light the dynamite, then lob it in through the
windows.

"When they explode, a few pigs might go up with them,"
he said. "The others'll panic and come running out. We
hole up on the other side of the road and pick 'em off.
Then we go in, down to the cellar. Break the cells open, set
everyone free. Then we vanish."

He reeled it all off lightly and it sounded dead simple.
But of course we knew it wasn't. It was anything but
simple, and if it went wrong, we'd be lucky if any of us
survived.

Everyone went silent again. Then I said to Flint that
he could count me in. I'd promised him: whatever he was
planning, I would be in on it. And I wanted to be there.
My hate was still so huge.

When Tom heard that, he joined in too. I don't know if
he was really convinced though. Maybe he just didn't want
to leave me alone. And Ferret was similar. He hesitated the
longest but in the end he said yes too.

So there were five of us last night. It was a starry, freezing cold night, and we took a roundabout route to Appellhofplatz. Didn't meet anyone, everywhere was deserted. When we got there, we hid behind a few big heaps of rubble opposite the EL-DE House, where we could see the entrance and the windows. There were lights on in several rooms on the first and second floors. We clenched our fists, cos we knew what happened up there.

We had the dynamite in our rucksacks. We'd tied it to bricks to make sure the windows would break when we threw it. Flint had divvied the sticks up and everyone had picked the window he'd aim at. Then we lit the fuses with military lighters we'd pinched. The minute everything was lit, we jumped up, ran over the road and lobbed the things.

By the time the windows shattered, we were already on our way back and taking cover again behind the rubble. Flint and Knuckles had their pistols at the ready, aimed at the door. Then we waited for the fireworks—but they didn't happen. I don't know if the dynamite had got damp or was lousy quality or if we just did something wrong. Anyway, not one of the sticks exploded.

Instead, the lights went on in every room. Orders were shouted, and then they started shooting at us from inside, on the upper floors. Flint and Knuckles returned fire and the rest of us kept our heads down. The bullets were just whistling round our ears and it got worse every second. Flint and Knuckles had to take cover too, and then the

Gestapo came out and started shooting at us from the entrance.

We had no choice but to beat it. Flint gave us a sign, then he and Knuckles let off another salvo and we ran for it. The Gestapo were shooting after us and took up the chase. We criss-crossed the streets. Jinked this way then that, but we couldn't get rid of them. Every time we thought we'd shaken them off, a new lot appeared from another direction and the whole thing started again.

We ended up surrounded on all sides and just managed to dive into the ruins of a bombed house. But then we were stuck there, couldn't go forwards or back. We were trapped and had to watch as the Gestapo men gathered outside.

"Tom, see if you can find any way out," Flint said. "We've got to get out of here before the area's sealed off. Best if you take Ferret with you. Gerlo needs to stay here. To reload."

Tom and Ferret went. We could see them vanish into the rubble, then we had to keep the Gestapo off our necks. Flint and Knuckles shot at anything moving on the street. But we couldn't stop them getting closer and closer. They'd got sub-machine guns, and in the long term we had no chance against them.

It seemed like half a lifetime before Tom and Ferret reappeared. But they'd got good news, they thought they'd found an escape route.

"Through the cellar," Tom whispered. "If we're quick, we can make it. Come on, let's go!"

He crawled away again with Ferret, I followed them. Then we noticed that Flint and Knuckles weren't with us. We turned back: they were still lying there, making no attempt to come with us.

"Flint!" Tom called. "We've got to go!"

Flint shooed him away. "Go without me," he said. "I'll hold 'em off a bit longer."

"That's madness, man! You can't do it alone."

"Then it's madness. But I've had enough, Tom. I'm not running away again."

We tried to convince him that he had to come with us. But there was nothing doing.

"Am I your Cap'n or not?" he asked.

"Yes, but…"

"And have I ever given you an order?"

"No, damn it."

"Well then, I've got an order going spare then. And this is it now, beat it!"

He turned away again and shot at the shadows that were moving towards us through the rubble. We could see them jumping over the stones and then taking cover again. They weren't far away now. Flint fired at them a couple of times, then he turned to Knuckles.

"That goes for you too, man!" he said. "Get lost!"

Knuckles shook his head. "Nah, Flint. I ain't goin' wivvout you. An' you can't do a fing about it."

Flint looked at him and there's no way of describing his expression. Then he took Knuckles's pistol, reloaded it and pressed it back into his hand.

"Get yourselves out of here!" he said to us. "We'll cover you."

What could we do? The shadows were getting ever closer, we had no time left. Tom said to Flint and Knuckles to come after us as soon as they could. Then we went.

Almost the minute we left, the two of them started shooting again. We ran on. Tom led us zigzagging through the rubble. Luckily he still found the way in the dark. It led to some stairs going down. They were half buried, but there was a crack we could crawl through. It had to be down there somewhere—the route they'd found.

We stopped and looked back. We could still see the flashes where Flint and Knuckles were as they fired, and hear the bang of their guns. But the rattle of the machine guns was louder. We could see the Gestapo jumping over the rubble and working their way up to them. And then their pistols suddenly went quiet, probably run out of ammo. A rabble of shadows appeared. The machine pistols rattled, we saw the flashes. Then it was quiet. Horribly quiet.

I was stunned, couldn't think. Tom pulled me on. We went down the crack into the cellar. Ferret had his torch on. It was devastation everywhere, partly collapsed, but there was a hole in the wall where we could climb into the next cellar, and then on. There are holes everywhere now. People knock them through so they can escape if their building *takes a direct hit. We got from one cellar to another, till there was no way on. Then we went up, kicked in a back door, and when we got out into the yard, it was on a completely different road. That's how we escaped before they sealed the area off.*

We still haven't really grasped what happened. I spent the whole day today waiting for Flint and Knuckles to come round a corner towards us somewhere. Someone like Flint wouldn't just let himself be blown away like that, I thought. Anyone else, but not him! No one could take him!

But of course they didn't come. And they never will come. We crouched together and somehow knew that it was the end of everything. Without Flint and Knuckles, there's no "us" left. It's over.

The best always go early, Tom said. That's why the world's so awful. I think he's right. It just had to end like this. Nothing else was possible. It's the only ending that fits for people like Flint and Knuckles.

Flint as an old man? I thought, as I replayed our time with him in my head. And then I had to laugh. Can't imagine it!

1st March 1945

The Edelweiss Pirates are no more. Our Cap'n is dead! There's no one left to steer the ship. Tom, Floss, Ferret and me: we're just four people trying to survive somehow. That's all—we've got nothing else left.

A couple of days ago, Ferret said he knew a place we could crawl into for a while. He'd been to his mum's to see how she was, and she told him. Said there's a church in the south of the city that's been ruined since last year but under it there's this ancient vault where the priest's been hiding Jews and deserters. And other people who're escaping the Nazis. And she knew how we could get in touch with him.

We didn't waste time thinking and went to see the priest. When he first heard our story, he didn't want to believe it. He looked us in the eyes for ages, one after another. Then he didn't ask any more questions, just took us in.

So the vault under the church has been our new home for three days now. There are a couple of dozen people hiding here, lots haven't seen daylight for months. Some don't speak, they've been through such terrible things. The priest and a couple of women from the parish look after them. Provide food and make sure no one tips over the edge.

Ferret's always had a bit of time for the church. He never talked about it much, probably a bit embarrassed, but he never denied it either. The rest of us aren't that interested in religion and that. Everything that's happened makes it kind of hard to believe in a God of love. But this priest and the women who help him are pretty decent. They'd do anything for the people down here. I reckon if this hideout got busted, they'd be standing right in front of them to get shot to pieces if they could save their lives that way. It does you good to see a thing like that. And then it doesn't really matter whether him upstairs is real or not.

In return for being allowed to sneak into the vault, we get cracking at night and round up a bit of grub for everyone. After all, we've got the experience, there's no flies on us. The priest is glad that we can give him a bit of a hand in that direction. He says stealing may be a sin, but in this case it's a good sin. Only we're not to tell him exactly how we do it, he doesn't want to know.

And we've found another job now too. A couple of days ago, one of the women had a little boy brought to her. She says he was wandering the streets in a daze after an air raid. Probably his family were killed and now he's all alone. The priest asked if we could look after him. Said he didn't have anyone else just now and it'd only be for a while, till they find a better solution.

Floss said yes at once and the rest of us had no objections. The kid's a bit unhinged and doesn't talk much—we don't even know his name—but we're sure he'll be a nice little chap once he's feeling better. And it's good to have him around. Things don't feel so pointless with him. Now there's something worthwhile again. Even if it's only small.

6th March 1945

Suddenly it's over—the war. The Allies were edging closer and closer, and now they're here. The army fled back across *the Rhine, and there's no sign of the Gestapo or the SS any more either. Overnight, they blew up the last few bridges that were still standing. So that nobody can follow them. Now they've vanished.*

Almost the moment we heard, we went up out of the vault and walked through the streets. What we saw was uncanny. Everywhere, people were crawling out of the rubble and the cellars like ghosts. Grey, with sunken faces and eyes like holes. Most of them just stood there, looking up at the sky. As if they couldn't believe they were still alive and that there'd be nothing bad coming from up there any more.

We ran to Ehrenfeld. American tanks were rolling into the city down Venloer. They were open, the soldiers were sitting up at the top, arms resting casually on the gun barrels. When they saw us at the side of the street, their eyes grew suspicious. No wonder, after they've had weeks of HJers leaping out at them with Panzerfausts. I felt uncertain. If only Flint was here, I thought. He'd know what to do. He'd know how to act around them!

We stood there for a while, watching the column of tanks. It was an endlessly long procession and somehow, everything suddenly seemed unreal to me. I'd been hoping for this day for so long. For the day when everything's over, when we're finally free and can breathe freely again. But now it was here, I suddenly felt helpless. I looked at the others and knew they were the same. What shall we do now? I thought. Where do we belong? And who actually are we?

I wonder if anyone'll be interested in what we did. Will anyone ever want to know? Or was it all pointless? Has it stopped mattering already?

Today's my eighteenth birthday. I didn't even think about it all day. I've only just remembered.

Old Mr Gerlach died before the winter came to an end. It was late at night, the nurse said, actually the early hours of the morning. The pain had stopped. He'd just gone to sleep and not woken up again.

The day after the funeral, I visited him at the cemetery. First, I stood at my grandad's grave and remembered seeing Mr Gerlach for the first time. He'd been over there, at his brother's grave. His own was right next to it. I went over and looked at it. "Josef Gerlach" it said on the stone. And beneath that: "6.3.1927–21.1.2012".

By then I also knew why he'd watched me so attentively that day. He'd left a letter for me, explaining it. The little boy, the one he and the others had taken in at the end of the war, had been my grandfather. Later, he'd gone to a foster family and never seen the Edelweiss Pirates again. Maybe that was the story he'd wanted to tell me before his death.

At any rate, Mr Gerlach had never forgotten the boy and had followed his life from a distance—inconspicuously, as was his way. That was how he'd heard about his death many decades later. And when my grandad was buried near his brother in the Ehrenfeld cemetery, he'd seen me and guessed that I was the grandson of the child he'd helped take care of. That's how it had begun—and so it came to an end in the same place.

As it started to snow, I stood there and remembered things old Mr Gerlach had written in his diary. There was one idea in particular that I couldn't get out of my head. He'd said it to Tilly—on that evening shortly before she died. That people like them needed nothing more than air to breathe, a path to walk down and a song to sing. I don't know why, but that sentence had stuck in my mind since I'd read it. Perhaps I should take it literally, I thought. The only thing was to find the right song.

The snow was falling more thickly. I pulled my hood over my head and crouched by the grave.

"Because it's so precious," I said and couldn't help smiling. Now I was doing exactly the thing that I'd found so strange about him: I was talking even though there was nobody around.

"Do you remember? I promised to tell you when I finished. Why I was reading it so slowly. That's the answer: because it's so precious."

The day before, I'd been in his flat for the last time. I'd collected the birds because I wanted to keep my promise to look after them. I'd also taken the music box. It seemed like a good idea to place it on his grave. I had the feeling he'd like that.

As I looked for a good place for it, I noticed that there were white flowers lying by the gravestone. They looked fresh, as if they'd only just been left there. Had someone already been here today? I stood up and looked around. And then I saw, a fair distance away, under the trees, the figure who'd been standing in the care-home garden.

When she saw me looking, she turned and hurried away. But before she got to the end of the cemetery and disappeared from sight, she stopped once more. She turned around and now I could see her face. It was an old woman. She was small and even from that distance, and through the falling snow, I could make out her cleft lip.

She hesitated, then she turned and left. My first thought was to run after her. But I didn't.

I just watched. And let her go.

21st May 1945

The worst winters are followed by the most beautiful springs. That's how it's been this year. Not a cloud to be seen for days. The sky shines so blue it hurts your eyes.

It's Whitsun, so we travelled to the Felsensee. With the kid we're looking after. There's no one here but us, we're all alone. It's a strange atmosphere, almost unreal. It's as though time's standing still, or we've landed in another world. No bombs ever fell on the lake, no soldiers' boots ever touched the shore. It's like the war never happened, as if all the dreadful things that happened elsewhere were just dreams from another life.

It dragged on almost two months after Cologne was liberated. Hundreds of thousands marched to their deaths. Totally pointlessly—for nothing. In the end, boys younger than us had to defend Berlin. Died like flies, people say. When everything was lost, Hitler killed himself. Then the military capitulated. Only *then. Because nobody had the guts before that.*

That was just over two weeks ago. Now we're sitting in the warm spring air. I'm up here on the cliff writing in my diary. I somehow managed to keep it safe through everything and now it's almost full. Tom and Floss are with the little one by the water, I can see them from here.

Ferret's roaming around somewhere cos he wants to see if he can find anything from the time when there were the big meetings here.

Whenever I remember that time, I find myself thinking about the others. The ones who aren't here any more. I can see them all around me. Lanky, who taught us so much. Goethe with his songs. Maja, who was always so sad. Knuckles, who wasn't rattled by anything. Flint, our Cap'n, who we admired so much. And Tilly!

Sometimes, for a moment, it's like the old days. Then everything comes to life. I can see everyone in their swashbuckling clothes, hear them laughing and singing, smell the campfire and feel the sun and the water and the sweat on my skin. And for a moment it's there again—that indescribable feeling that we had back then.

But it never lasts long, it passes and everything disappears again. There's nobody there but us and everything's quiet. All you can hear are the birds—and the kid down at the shore. He's started talking again, sometimes he babbles away to himself like he's got to catch up with everything he missed over the last few weeks. He won't be with us much longer, one of the women from the parish will take him in. And that's fine. She'll take better care of him than we could.

But a name—we ought to give him that. He can't remember his old one, you see—or doesn't want to. I just had an idea. I found myself thinking about that book, about Robinson Crusoe, who was stranded on a desert *island. We were something like that here at the Felsensee, shipwrecked pirates on a desert island. And the kid's lost his ship too. So why not name him after that? But Robinson isn't a good name—everyone would take the mick. We could name him after the author of the book, Daniel, he was called. Yeah, why not? I'll suggest it to the others.*

Ferret's just coming back from his walk round the lake. It's nearly time to head home. We didn't talk about it much—we're really here for a kind of goodbye, I suppose. I don't think we'll ever come back again. It's better not to mess up the memories.

We'll stay a few more minutes, then we've got to go. To be honest, I'm scared of that. The years behind us were awful—and yet so incredibly good. We'll never get them back, and the moment we leave the lake, they'll be over for ever.

Because it was here. Here in this place that we found it. In its purest and noblest form, that we only see in the darkest times:

Our freedom.

AFTERWORD

These youths, aged 12–17, loll around here until the late hours of the evening with musical instruments and young females. [...] It is suspected that these youths are the ones who write "Down with Hitler", "The OKW [Armed Forces High Command] are liars", "Medals and orders for wholesale slaughter", "Down with the Nazi Beast", etc. These inscriptions may be removed as often as one likes, but within a few days, the walls have been written on again. [...] Although the young people know that it is forbidden to linger in the Ostpark late in the evening, they are constantly reappearing and consistently do so around the weekends. As well as nocturnal disturbances, they display provocative behaviour. The local residents complain about this and rightly so. It is crucial to undertake something in this matter and I request that appropriate steps be taken against this rabble.

This was the "distress call" with which the Nazi *Ortsgruppenleiter* for Düsseldorf-Grafenberg turned to the Gestapo and demanded tougher action against teenagers opposed to the regime, which included the "Edelweiss Pirates" movement. These groups of young people were widespread throughout the cities in the Rhine and Ruhr area during the Second World War; their numbers were highest in Cologne, but they could also be encountered in Düsseldorf, Wuppertal, Essen, Dortmund, Duisburg and many other cities. The Hitler Youth (*Hitlerjugend*, HJ), SS and Gestapo waged a regular running battle against them, but never got them truly under control. We can still only estimate the total numbers of teenagers in the movement but, towards the end of the war, it must certainly have been several thousand.

This means that the characters in this book—the young people around Gerlo and Flint—are invented, but only up to a point because they are similar to the "real" Edelweiss Pirates. The same goes for their experiences, which are based on what former members of the movement wrote in their memoirs—sometimes many decades later—and described in conversations. The hardships that working-class teenagers suffered in the HJ, the secret meetings in parks, such as the Volksgarten in Cologne, weekend trips into the countryside and to the Felsensee, the battles with the HJ, being stalked by the HJ patrols, daubing slogans on walls, distributing leaflets, interrogation and torture by the Gestapo, including by Hoegen and Kütter in the EL-DE House, going underground and being considered "illegals", and finally committing attacks with firearms and dynamite—all these things are described by former Edelweiss Pirates in their autobiographies. As well as these,

I used a range of other sources for this book, including academic literature, archive materials, contemporary diaries and newspaper articles.

The story of the Edelweiss Pirates was not over in 1945, however. Although the gangs largely broke up after the end of the war, and no longer had any major role to play, the way they were dealt with shines a telling light on the understanding of history in the Federal Republic of Germany* and how it has changed. Until the 1970s and even the 80s, the prevailing view was that the Edelweiss Pirates had not been an opposition group, let alone resistance fighters, but mere teenage criminals and troublemakers. The claim for compensation made by the family of Bartholomäus Schink gives us a typical example of this view.

"Barthel", as his friends called him, was only sixteen when he was publicly hanged on 10th November 1944 in Hüttenstrasse, near Ehrenfeld station, along with five other Edelweiss Pirates, who had gone underground following persecution by the Gestapo. In 1954, his mother applied to the president of Cologne's regional government to have her son recognized as a victim of political persecution. In 1962, the authorities rejected the application on the grounds that the Edelweiss Pirates had been only a "band of criminals". This assessment was based on witness statements from former Gestapo officials Hirschfeld and

* This was the formal name of West Germany before reunification in 1990 and of Germany today. History teaching and coming to terms with the Nazi past were handled very differently in the old Communist East Germany.

Hoegen, while no importance was given to statements by surviving Edelweiss Pirates.

It was not until 1978 that the Edelweiss Pirates' reputation began to be rehabilitated, when an article in the magazine *Monitor* pointed out that Bartholomäus Schink was still entered in court records as a "criminal". This was followed by a citizens' initiative in Ehrenfeld, set up to correct this assessment. Songs and plays were written and the first academic works on the Edelweiss Pirates were published.

In 1984, Albert Klütsch, a member of the North Rhine-Westphalia state parliament for the Social Democratic Party (SPD), applied to have the Edelweiss Pirates officially recognized as resistance fighters. The then Minister of the Interior, Herbert Schnoor, commissioned a report from the historian Peter Hüttenberger. Bernd Rusinek, Hüttenberger's PhD student, published the study in 1988 and came to the conclusion that while the Edelweiss Pirates had not been criminals, they were not "genuine" resistance fighters either. Many former Edelweiss Pirates who had survived the war and persecution by the Nazi regime considered this judgement discriminatory.

So how should we actually assess the Edelweiss Pirates? It is clear that they did not have a comprehensive political vision like the 20th July conspirators, they were not intellectuals like the members of the White Rose, they were not politically organized like the members of the communist resistance, and they did not have the moral authority of a

Dietrich Bonhoeffer or a Cardinal von Galen. But how can anyone demand that of them? They were just working-class teenagers, mostly from broken families, with precisely eight years of compulsory education behind them, who had been thrown into the machinery of the war economy at the age of just fourteen. Where should they have acquired a developed political consciousness from? They had nothing more than sound common sense and an elementary sense of good and evil, right and wrong.

As a result, most of them were not political resistance fighters at the beginning. They just wanted their freedom, objected to being pushed around, wanted to have their own say about their lives and to do what they felt like doing. At first, they were rebelling not against the Nazis as such, but against all authorities that they felt were oppressing them and hemming them in. But this forced them into conflict with the institutions of the Nazi regime. And it was at this point that many of them started to develop a political awareness. They recognized the injustice around them and turned against it.

Mind you, this does not apply to all of them: there was no such thing as "the" Edelweiss Pirates. Rather than a clearly structured organization with a constitution and a manifesto, it was a movement of many hundreds of small, local groupings, each of which developed in its own way. Some never turned to political resistance and stuck to their rather apathetic phase of youthful rebellion. Similarly, after the war, some of them were as fiercely opposed to institutions set up by the occupying powers as they had been to Nazi authorities.

But over time, others—and they are the subject of this book—developed a political consciousness that was fed not by theoretical considerations but by practical experience. They grasped the unjust nature of the Nazi regime and, from there on, moved beyond mere defiance and rejection of authority. Think of the actions that the authors mentioned above describe in their memoirs. Or the leaflet by Edelweiss Pirates from Wuppertal in September 1942, which led to the first major raid against the movement. It was headed: "To the enslaved youth of Germany" and contained the poem: "Soon will come the day, when we're free again. When we cast off every chain. When there's no more need to hide the songs we sing inside." The text ran: "German youth, rise up and fight for the freedom and rights of your children and children's children. Because if Hitler wins the war, Europe will be in chaos, the world will be enslaved until Judgement Day. Put an end to this slavery before it's too late. Lord set us free!" Can there be any doubt that this is a case of political resistance?

Rusinek's report contained the criticism that campaigns of this kind did not come from the teenagers themselves, but that they had been virtually forced into them by circumstances. But weren't the 20th July plotters also "driven" into their actions by the realities they came across? And can't the same also be said of the White Rose? Besides, the Nazis themselves were never in any doubt about the character of the Edelweiss Pirates: the Gestapo were concerned with them from early on, and later it was almost exclusively they who dealt with them—in Cologne this even extended to setting up a dedicated task force to tackle them. And it is well-known that the Gestapo were responsible for political opponents, not ordinary criminals.

So why were the Edelweiss Pirates defamed as criminals for decades? Perhaps people didn't want to accept that a gang of kids could have opposed the Nazis so bravely, because they hadn't dared to do so themselves. Besides, defiant working-class teenagers did not fit the picture of the resistance. Resistance was seen as—always—having come from the elites. People denied the mere possibility of resistance from below, from ordinary people. Because what would that possibility have meant for the silent majority who always swam with the tide?

After 1945, everyone was faced with the reality of the Nazi regime and its crimes, and had to explain that reality, and their own involvement in it—to themselves above all. So it was easiest to say: we didn't know a thing and we couldn't have done a thing. People repeated it for so long that they ended up believing it themselves. The Edelweiss Pirates interfered with their ability to reassure themselves that they had been innocent. People refused to believe them. They didn't want to admit that people like them could even have existed. They made life easy for themselves by degrading them to petty criminals, yobs and hooligans. They were simply *Krade*—scum.

It was not until the 1980s that a more nuanced picture began to develop. For the first time, there was recognition that it had not only been members of a noble elite who fought against Nazism, but that there had also been acts of resistance among the general population. Most of them have never been known, and never will be. All the same, their moral value is no less than that of the 20th July conspirators or the White Rose. The thing that they show most clearly is this: people *could* know things—if they opened their eyes. And they *could* do something—if they had the courage.

The official vindication of the Edelweiss Pirates came after the turn of the millennium. On 9th November 2003, a memorial plaque to the executed Edelweiss Pirates was unveiled in Ehrenfeld—on the part of Hüttenstrasse that is now called Bartholomäus-Schink-Strasse. And on 16th June 2005, 60 years after the end of the war, Jürgen Roters, the president of Cologne's regional government, officially recognized the Ehrenfeld Edelweiss Pirates as resistance fighters at a ceremony in the district government building.

It might well have begun as almost harmless youthful recalcitrance, but the Edelweiss Pirates had the courage and decency to stand up against an unjust regime, and they would not be thrown off that course, even by brutal persecution. They were part of the other, better, Germany. We should not stop telling their story.

GLOSSARY

20th July conspirators: The leaders of the plot to kill Hitler on 20th July 1944, led by Colonel Claus von Stauffenberg.

Block Warden: Officially called *Blockleiter* (Block Leaders), these were low-ranking Nazi officials whose job was to supervise a neighbourhood and report suspicious behaviour to the authorities.

Brownshirts (SA): Members of the SA (short for *Sturmabteilung*, meaning "assault division") were known as the Brownshirts because of the colour of their uniform. It was a violent paramilitary group formed in 1921. The Brownshirts were prominent in Hitler's rise to power, but gradually lost influence and were superseded by the SS after 1934.

Cardinal von Galen: Roman Catholic Bishop of Münster from 1933 who protested against some Nazi policies, denounced the Gestapo and criticized the persecution of the church. He was put under virtual house arrest in 1941.

Coming-of-age ceremony: Officially called the *Verpflichtung der Jugend* (Day of Youth Commitment), this was intended to replace religious ceremonies such as confirmation, and mark the time when a boy went up from the junior section into the full Hitler Youth.

"Could call him Meier": In a speech to the German air force in September 1939, Hermann Göring said: "No enemy bomber can reach the Ruhr. If one reaches the Ruhr, my name is not Göring. You can call me Meier." As the young Gerlach notes, people did take to calling him Meier, and air raid sirens were sometimes also known as "Meier's Trumpets".

Dietrich Bonhoeffer: Lutheran pastor and theologian. He was a prominent opponent of the Nazis from the beginning and was involved in setting up the Confessing Church, a Protestant church opposed to the official pro-Nazi Protestant Reich Church. He was executed in 1945.

EL-DE House: The Gestapo headquarters in Cologne. It originally belonged to a jeweller, Leopold Dahmen, and took its name from his initials. It is now a museum and memorial, the National Socialist Documentation Centre.

Führer: This was the title adopted by Hitler as leader of the Nazi Party in 1921. It means "leader". When Hitler first came to power in Germany, he was appointed Chancellor (equivalent to Prime Minister) while Hindenburg remained as President. On Hindenburg's death, the positions of Chancellor and President were merged, and

Hitler took the title *Führer und Reichskanzler* before the Chancellor part was dropped. Many other ranks within the political, military and paramilitary organizations also featured the term.

Gestapo: The official secret police, short for *Geheime Staatspolizei* (Secret State Police). They were responsible for repressing opponents of the Nazi regime as well as having a major involvement in the Holocaust. They were feared because of their brutal methods and the fact that they wore plain clothes.

Grohé: Josef Grohé was a senior Nazi official. He was *Gauleiter* (regional party leader) for the Cologne-Aachen area and became *Reichskommissar* (Reich Commissioner) for Belgium and Northern France in 1944.

"Heil Hitler!" (Hail Hitler!): The required greeting in Nazi Germany. "Heil" could also mean "heal" so when the Edelweiss Pirates wanted to shock people by not using the proper salute, they responded by saying: "No, heal him yourself!"

Hitler Youth: The *Hitlerjugend* (HJ) was the only permitted youth organization in Nazi Germany. Children were required to join on 20th April (Hitler's birthday) in the year they turned ten. Boys aged 10–14 joined the *Jungvolk* (Young Folk) and girls joined the *Jungmädel* (Young Girls) before moving up to the senior organizations.

Jungstammführer: The Hitler Youth and *Jungvolk* had similar hierarchies to other Nazi organizations. A

Jungstammführer was a young adult, in charge of a group of companies within the *Jungvolk*.

Jungvolk: The section of the Hitler Youth for younger children. *Jungvolk* means "Young Folk" or "Young People", and recruits were known as *Pimpfen*, a slang word for a boy or little rascal. They did activities such as camping, sports and hiking, but there was also military training and political indoctrination.

League of German Girls: The *Bund Deutscher Mädel* (BDM) was the girls' wing of the Hitler Youth.

Night of Broken Glass: On 9th and 10th November 1938, Jewish homes, businesses and synagogues were attacked across Germany. It was known in German as *Kristallnacht* (Crystal Night) and in English as the Night of Broken Glass because so many windows were smashed. Many Jewish people were killed or arrested.

Ortsgruppenleiter (**Local Group Leader**): The Nazi leader of a large town, city or district.

Ostarbeiter: This term, meaning "Eastern Worker", was given to foreign workers from Eastern and Central Europe brought to Germany to do slave labour in factories, on farms and in private households. They were both men and women and were often housed in labour camps. They were forbidden to socialize or have any contact with Germans.

Panzerfaust: Literally "tank fist", this was a single-shot anti-tank weapon similar to a bazooka. It was a small, pre-loaded tube that fired a high-explosive warhead. By the end of the war, they were being used by teenage HJ boys to try to hold back Allied tanks.

Patrols: The Hitler Youth *Streifendienst* (Patrol Service) was a kind of internal police force to maintain order within the HJ and report disloyalty.

Pimpfenprobe: The initiation test for boys joining the *Jungvolk*.

Platoon Leader (*Jungzugführer*): Groups of ten boys within the *Jungvolk* were called a *Jungenschaft*, with leaders chosen from the older boys; four of these formed a unit called a *Jungzug* or platoon.

Radio Nippes: Humorous name for the BBC in Cologne. Nippes is a district in northern Cologne. In earlier centuries it was outside the city walls and thus was also used as a joke name for "abroad".

Reichsbahn: The German State Railway.

Reichstag: The German parliament and its building in Berlin. On 27th February 1933, the Reichstag building was burned down. A Dutch communist was accused of starting the fire and this gave Hitler an excuse to have the Communist Party officials arrested. After the March elections, the Communist Party was banned.

Siegfried Line: Known in German as the Westwall, this was a line of defences including tunnels, bunkers and tank traps running almost 400 miles along the western border of Germany. It was built in the 1930s and in need of major restoration in 1944.

SS: Short for *Schutzstaffel* (Protection Squadron). Initially a small group of Hitler's personal bodyguards, it became a major military and paramilitary organization. The SS was responsible for policing, racial policy and the concentration and extermination camps.

Strafing: Attacking a target on the ground from a low-flying aircraft.

Völkischer Beobachter: The Nazi Party daily newspaper; it was violently anti-Semitic and a key source of Nazi propaganda.

Volkssturm: The home guard established in October 1944 and made up largely of old men and young boys.

White Rose (*Weisse Rose*): A resistance group led by a group of students from the University of Munich. They used leaflets and graffiti to call for opposition to the Nazi regime. The leaders were arrested by the Gestapo in February 1943. Hans and Sophie Scholl and Christoph Probst were executed shortly afterwards.

Youth Movement: The German Youth Movement was founded in 1896. It consisted of various young people's associations, including the Scouts and hiking groups such as the *Wandervogel*. Some of these groups were opposed to the Nazis and therefore banned, while others were incorporated into the Hitler Youth.

THE LETTER FOR THE KING
THE SECRETS OF THE WILD WOOD
THE SONG OF SEVEN
THE GOLDSMITH AND THE MASTER THIEF

Tonke Dragt

HOW TO BE BRAVE

Daisy May Johnson

RED STARS

Davide Morosinotto

LAMPIE

Annet Schaap

THE MISSING BARBEGAZZI
THE HUNGRY GHOST

H.S. Norup

THE TUNNELS BELOW

Nadine Wild-Palmer

SCHOOL FOR NOBODIES
THE THREE IMPOSSIBLES

Susie Bower

THE ELEPHANT

Peter Carnavas